Peaces

Peaces

HELEN
OYEYEMI

faber

This edition first published in the UK in 2021
by Faber & Faber Limited
Bloomsbury House
74–77 Great Russell Street
London WC1B 3DA

First published in the United States in 2021
by Riverhead Books
an imprint of Penguin Random House LLC
penguinrandomhouse.com

Printed in the UK by CPI Group (UK) Ltd, Croydon CR0 4YY

Quote by Ludvík Vaculík found on page 142 is courtesy of Gerald
Turner's translation of *A Czech Dreambook*, published by Karolinum
Press in 2019.

A CIP record for this book
is available from the British Library

ISBN 978–0–571–36657–6

2 4 6 8 10 9 7 5 3 1

I many times thought peace had come,

When peace was far away;

As wrecked men deem they sight the land

At centre of the sea,

And struggle slacker, but to prove,

As hopelessly as I,

How many the fictitious shores

Before the harbor lie.

—Emily Dickinson

Peaces

1.

Have you ever had an almost offensively easy breakup? The kind where the person you've just broken ties with because of blah blah and blah gives you a slight shrug, a "Thanks for everything—especially your honesty," then walks away whistling Hoagy Carmichael's "I Get Along Without You Very Well"? Or has that been you—the low-key dumpee? I've never once taken it on the chin like that, never even thought of trying to. Before Honza I'd only been with similarly emotive types: we could've formed a tribe of some sort, united under a banner that read FOREVER REJECTING YOUR REJECTION. But this . . . this was just ten uncomfortable minutes in a coffee shop. Then it was done, Honza had left, and I was all grateful and relieved that we'd kept it civil. I thought: *So that's it, then. It's all over.*

I put in my earphones and walked to the tube station with my brain slurping up my bright new beginnings playlist like syrup. The music put me in such a good mood that when the sneaky hand of a pickpocket settled on my backpack I just slapped it away and shook a finger at him instead of grabbing him and hurling him down the escalator.

There were no messages from Honza when I got home. All that remained of the relationship was a set of boxer shorts he'd given me. Tapestry-print days-of-the-week boxers with the crucial information embroidered in crimson thread across the waistband of each pair: *Pondělí, Úterý, Středa* . . . He claimed it made him sad that I always seem to think it's Monday. And look—now I knew seven words of Czech! I'd be fluent in no time, he said.

The post-breakup days trooped by. I worked, I volunteered, I watched some shows, read some books, saw some friends, wore my set of tapestry-print underwear in the usual order. Pondělí, no wistful question or maudlin plea, Úterý, no by-the-way-you're-full-of-shit essay, Středa, no saw-this-and-thought-of-you photo, Čvrtek, no offer of a chance to change my mind, Pátek, Sobota, Neděle, no nothing. A cycle repeated for months until the underwear had been washed and worn to rags. Binning that gift set seemed to conclude our conscious uncoupling process (the worst of it is I think I might be only half joking), though it wasn't long before I missed the perfection of fit and invested in more of the same. There were a lot of different language options I could have pursued for my new days-of-the-week underwear, but I sought security, not novelty, so I stuck with the original formula. People may betray you, but the right pair of boxers—never. As for Honza Svoboda, I didn't hear another word from or about him, until. Until—

2.

I haven't even started and I'm already losing my nerve. OK, I'll get on with it, before I change my mind.

Picture it—about four years later, a starry-eyed young couple takes a trip on a sleeper train . . .

Xavier laughs at the idea of thirty-eight being considered young. That's how old we both were at the time, though. And, overall, not so mature in terms of conduct.

Anyway:

Our local train station is typical of a small village transport hub in deepest Kent. It's the first and last stop for the village's two bus routes, and no matter how determined we passengers are to simply pass through, we tarry. The building has a dishevelled magnetism to it, striking the senses as an overgrown cousin of a country barn. A cousin conversant with the infernal. There it is (the workaday infernal), smoking away in the fade of the exterior paint, and there it is again in the gaslit appearance of each window frame, those shadows that shrink behind the sepia glass. You could just about believe that Lucifer's got a few ham hocks strung up in there, and that he visits every now and then to see for himself how far along in the curing process they've come. But in place of hellish hams there's a station café that serves UNESCO World Heritage–level cuppas. To round it all off there are two train tracks, where four times a day departing and arriving passengers mingle with the villagers who've come to welcome them or see them off. Two arrivals and two departures every twenty-four hours isn't quite enough for a railway track to seriously devote itself to being what people say it is . . . As per our instructions, we were at the station at half past six on a Saturday morning in spring, and the honeysuckle, butterflies, and other revellers didn't seem too concerned about the comings and goings of the trains. I suppose all the pretty tumbling and fluttering and flapping and whatnot marked them out as ambassadors of the season and secured them right of way.

The train was waiting on the London-bound track, looking more like a seafaring creature than a locomotive. Our companion at the time was a mongoose named Árpád, and he bristled at the sight of it. "See the dragon, see its mane," I whispered to him. Sleek scrolls of silvered metal flickered and twisted their way all along its long, low body. The train bore its name like a diadem, scarlet letters dancing along a ruby red band set just above the window of the driver's cabin. T H E L U C K Y D A Y.

The driver's cabin was empty. Árpád examined the station platform, patting the concrete with his paws as if preparing to launch himself into the air and fall upon his foe.

Xavier told Árpád he was overreacting and yet, from where

we stood, it looked as if the wheels had tucked themselves over the rail tracks. *See its mane, see its claws . . .*

All I said was: "Bling a ling a ling. A tad conspicuous for a tea-smuggling train, isn't it?"

A passerby wearing a high-visibility jacket and a yellow hard hat asked if we were off anywhere nice. I said, "No idea, mate," but Xavier draped an arm around me and informed her that we were off on our non-honeymoon honeymoon. An answer that made this life event of ours a destination in and of itself at the same time as downplaying the fact that we really didn't know if we were going anywhere nice. The wording on our ticket was the vaguest conceivable. Árpád may have been unhappy about that, but we non-honeymoon honeymooners didn't much care.

We strolled the platform more or less in step for a while, Xavier and I, and we indulged in a bit of sentimental murmuring. I barely recall what it was we said to each other—I'm sure it was classic "is this real life"–type commentary—it was the sound of his voice and the sweet sting of his glance that hurt me in ways only he could kiss better. You run the romantic gauntlet for decades without knowing who exactly it is you're giving and taking such a battering in order to reach. You run the gauntlet without knowing whether the person whose favour you seek will even be there once you somehow put that path strewn with sensory confetti and emotional gore behind you. And then, by some stroke of fortune, the gauntlet concludes, the person does exist after all, and you become that perpetually astonished lover from so many of the songs you used to find endlessly disingenuous.

It *was* really happening. We really had found each other, and we really were going away together—not for the first time, but for the first time travelling under a shared surname. This was to take place aboard a train called *The Lucky Day*. The train was there, and we were there, and so we kept saying things like "This is it," and "Here we go," as if trying to place verbal reins on the momentum of it all.

Each carriage door was sealed with a symbol. A dagger, a bumblebee, a spinning wheel, a harp. Our ticket placed us in Clock Carriage, so we began looking for a clock shape cast in the same dull brass as the others—a tulip, a telescope, a die that had rolled the number two . . .

We couldn't pass up the prospect of an onboard gambling den. The dice seal was pressed, but the door only opened at the third or fourth try; the first attempt was mine, Xavier went next, then Árpád, then me again. The two dots on the face of the dice weren't just adornment—you had to dip your fingers into them and really press. We all bundled into the carriage to have a look, taking our luggage with us so that we could roll it through other carriages as we looked for ours. And we hunched over, heads lowered and shoulders bowed—at least Xavier and I did—once it became fully apparent what an upside-down sort of place we'd entered. All the seats and tables were scattered across the ceiling among the luggage racks, looking very much as if they'd settled there after the train had undertaken a particularly vigorous loop-the-loop. The silence had a thin skin. We heard the rattle and chatter of the station, and a woolly murmur that may have been sleep talk from the train's engine. A normalising mesh of sound. We weren't in the correct carriage, but we weren't disturbing anything. And we in turn would not be disturbed . . . as long as we moved on. If you stuck out your tongue it would dance there, right at the tip: the fizz of conditionality. But Xavier seemed less fazed by this carriage than by something he saw in the next one. I followed his gaze but only saw a row of closed compartments.

Árpád trekked up the wall, did a tabletop dash across the ceiling, subjected us to a somewhat professorial gaze, as if to say, "And that's how exploring is done, kids," then slid to the ground and ambled back out onto the open air. I made to follow him but changed course when I saw Xavier headed for the door that led to the next compartment.

"Árpád went the other way," I said, slipping in between Xavier and the door handle.

"I know, but—"

"You know, but you're already trying to ditch us before we've even left the station?"

"Otto, it's a train, not the Yorkshire moors. We don't have to huddle together like hikers lost in the mists."

Our faces were very close together, but we didn't kiss. We'd moved, apparently of our own accord, into the exact spot where the weight of that crowded ceiling felt least balanced. Long-backed chairs hovered above our skulls, our wheeled luggage skittered across the bare floor, and I didn't know about Xavier, but I didn't dare break our pose. For that was how our bodies were arranged in relation to each other: lovers on the brink of a steamy clinch. I was the coy one, my left hand gripping the sun-warmed windowsill. Xavier's right hand was pressed to the door behind me, his wrist tickling the top of my ear. I could very easily have turned my head and touched my lips to his wrist, but I could see there was no competing with the view over my shoulder. I'd already lost him to the dim net of doors that ran through the centre of the train.

"You can't imagine how I longed for this day," I said. "And it's finally here. The day I officially become less fanciable than a door."

"Hmmm?" Looking down, he moved his hands over me. Slowly, so that I gasped. He said: "I like that sound. Not a sound that doors tend to make." But then he added: "I think I saw her, Otto."

"Her?"

I twisted around and tried to see for myself. The outline of each door fit so neatly into the ones that followed it that my eyesight, not particularly hardworking at the best of times, almost immediately let me down. There might have been someone, that could have been a shape moving around in one of the rectangles further back, but—

"You said 'her' as if I'm meant to know who she is."

"Ava."

"Ava . . . ?"

"Ava Kapoor."

After a couple of seconds of cold observation while I struggled to look like someone who was in the know, Xavier said: "Come on, Otto. Ava Kapoor. The resident."

"Right, of course. Ava *Kapoor*. Yeah. You . . . you think you saw her?"

"Well, I definitely saw someone."

"What was she like? Did she seem . . ."

Which words matched my hopes for how Ava Kapoor seemed? Amiable? Tranquil? In possession of all her marbles? I'd read a kind and practical letter of invitation from her, so I don't know why I anticipated an encounter with a Miss Havisham type. I'd like to know what it is that makes that disbelief so rigid. The one concerning women who live by themselves, I mean. Even though I know several, and even though I understand that for five out of seven of the female loners I know, it's truly their choice, the next female loner I meet never benefits from these other friendships I share, because at the moment our paths cross I instantly revert to *Oh God, what ails this person??*

Xavier said: "What was she like? I don't know. I don't know what you're even asking, Otto. But she held up a sign. Well, a word she'd written on a piece of paper."

He paused. "I think it said HELLO."

"OK . . ."

"But it could also have said HELP."

"It could also . . . have said HELP?"

"If you don't stop echoing me, Otto Montague . . . I mean Shin . . ."

"It's just— Listen, if you had to decide right now what the sign said, which would you lean towards? Did it say HELLO, or did it say HELP?"

Xavier raised his hand to his mouth, dropped it. "HELP. I think. But she didn't seem frantic. She came out of there"—he pointed towards the last compartment in the next carriage—"held up the sign, then . . . I think she shrugged? A 'never mind' sort of shrug. And she switched carriages."

"Was she . . . dressed all in white?"

"What? How does that affect our decision?"

"Our— OK, keep your hair on . . . what decision?"

"What do you think we should do about Ava Kapoor either saying hello or asking for help, Otto? Since I'm banned from acting as an individual."

"Glad you understand the ground rules for this trip . . . Well, we return the greeting, obviously. Or if it was the other thing, then we help."

"Exactly what I hoped you'd say. Where's Árpád?"

The carriage door was still open. There was our tidy little train station, not yet gone away. There was the green mist of the hedgerows and the gunpowder pop of petals. And there was Árpád's tail, beckoning us back onto the platform with its languorous rope dance. We hauled ourselves and our cases back out into the open air and resumed our walk along the outside of the train, peering in at carriage windows as we went by, occasionally opening a door in order to stick our heads in and whisper: "Hello? Ms. Kapoor? Hello?" Nobody answered, and Xavier put on a caffeine-deficient yet wine-rich daytime television presenter voice to ask: "Who lives . . . in a house like this?" All we saw were empty seats and curtains drawn across the glass.

As for Clock Carriage . . . did it even exist . . . perhaps we'd missed the symbol. "Clocks come in a variety of forms," I heard myself saying. "There are water clocks, for instance, and sundials . . ."

Then, at last: our carriage seal. There were roman numerals on it, and the complex cutwork you see on the faces of astronomical clocks. With ten minutes to departure (five minutes, really, to decide whether to let this train leave without us), Xavier and Árpád went in, while I waited on the platform with our worldly goods.

One minute, two minutes, three—they thumped by, second by second, I heard and saw them on the face of my watch. Such a noisy, glaring watch, compared to the shimmering stillness of *The Lucky Day.* I scanned the windows for faces—none appeared. I leaned in at the door, looking left, the direction man and mongoose had chosen. I called out the portmanteau name they both hated. One way or another it was bound to get a reaction. "Xárpád?"

The corridor was dark, but it shone like a water droplet. Satin and chrome, and no sound, no sound, then a great gale. Paws and hands and feet scrabbling. The door to a compartment midway down the corridor slid open, and Xavier looked out. "Otto, I have a feeling it's nice in here, but we won't know for sure until we find the light switch . . ."

I had been thinking of the train as a selective entity, welcoming Xárpád and discarding me. I'd only just forced myself to laugh at that thought and taken two mocking steps in Xárpád's direction (what a pair . . . unable to locate a light switch between them) when the floor hummed and the corridor swung forward with a hiss, compacting slightly, as if shedding excess bulk via pinpricked holes. We were off. I pulled Xavier's suitcase in with us just as the carriage door slid past the platform, and Xavier, at

my side the instant the train began to move, grabbed the handle
of Árpád's case. That was the best we could do. I looked back,
just once, to see my own suitcase lying on its side at the edge of
the track. I was wearing my Sobota boxers, but the next four
days were already lost.

3.

You should know that the train ride was a gift from one Shin Do Yeon. Her nephew had offered to share his surname with me, and I'd managed to accept with sedate joy, like a person who was in a normal amount of love. I might even have managed to ask if he was sure this was what he wanted. Not at all like the real me, who'd been putting my first name and his surname together over and over and over on various pieces of scrap paper ever since I'd met him. Three years of practice signatures.

He frowned at the deed poll document when it came through. "Should we have done it the other way around, so I'd have been Francis Xavier Montague?" he asked. There was no point answering until he'd thought about it all over again, so I just waited. After a long moment he looked up from the paper and said my new name with a satisfied nod. "Otto Shin . . ."

He brushed the back of his hand against my cheek. Heady stuff, that overlapping of live patterns, the subtle chequering of his hand. Rough and smooth, flexible knuckles and leathered skin.

His is the hand of a sea swimmer; in water it becomes a broad bladed oar. That same hand is a hardy aid to him as a once-a-week football goalie more enthusiastic than he is adept, and it's the fine-fingered hand the needle glitters from as it sews all the buttons back onto our shirts. This is only the preface to the prologue of the dossier on Xavier Shin's hands. For the rest, see Puccini's "*O dolci mani.*"

Do Yeon-ssi cleared her throat. "Hi, lovebirds," she said. "Yes, it's me again. Your aunt. I'm here too, remember? Why not take these train tickets and call it a honeymoon? It would've made me very happy if you'd done things properly and actually got married instead of this deed poll business. But there's no need to suddenly start caring about my happiness now when you never did before . . ."

Celebratory travel aside, there were also Árpád's needs to consider. Do Yeon-ssi wanted to make a special point of reminding us that Árpád XXX was getting on for six years old, and that it was very important for mongooses to travel before they reach middle age: "Otherwise they get narrow-minded."

This discussion took place in Do Yeon-ssi's study, where Árpád's favourite sandbox was located. We took a look at him and at the various bits of carefully polished treasure he was in the process of hiding. Back when it'd just been me and Árpád in my studio flat, he hadn't had many high-value items to look after. A bronze-coloured bottle top here and there, perhaps. But ever since Árpád XXX had become part of the Shin household, there were solid gold bracelets, diamond stud earrings, and jade rings. Árpád was clearly delighted with his hoard. I also saw signs of self-consciousness, which were fairly understandable, given that we'd all stopped talking and were now staring at him.

Árpád Montague XXX: well worth staring at. Notable features include his coat of platinum fur and the exceptionally well-sculpted length of his paws and feet—the grace of those alone might convince you Nijinsky's been reincarnated in mongoose form. Some snootiness of manner might be justified, and yet you could search the universe and fail to find a friendlier creature, or a fellow more willing to hear both sides of a story and disperse the benefit of the doubt in both directions if needed. During my more rational hours of the day—eleven in the morning, for instance, or three o'clock in the afternoon—I realise what I sound like when I talk about Árpád. I do realise it, and I know no one should listen to a word I say about him. The trouble is, I see all sorts of stories in that mongoose. He's a friend of two hundred years and more. By which I mean that he is his very own self and also every fit of laughter his predecessors have induced in mine, every ounce of liability, bewilderment, solace, simple certainty . . . Árpád XXX, the pick of Árpád XXIX's litter. And who was Árpád XXIX? Not only the most sardonic bosom friend of my teens and early twenties, but my mum's favourite of Árpád XXVIII's offspring. The twenty-eighth of our Árpáds would close his eyes and quiver ardently upon hearing certain lines of *Ulysses*. Tennyson's biggest fan.

Or was he?

Lieselotte (my mum) pointed out that Árpád XXVIII may

well have been trolling Martha (also my mum). Martha's the Montague descendant, and she's also one of those literature professors with a "postmodernism or goodbye" stance. She finds Victorian literature cloying at best, so all you have to do is recite a few lines of mid- to late-nineteenth-century poetry before her body language indicates she isn't coping. It would've been the easiest thing in the world for Árpád XXVIII to pick up on that.

I could write a book about the Árpáds, but I'll keep it to a couple of paragraphs. Árpád the First appeared one night in my great-grandfather's nursery when he was a very small boy in Kuching, Borneo. I'm sure almost no one deludes themselves that all their ancestors were decent. Pick a vein, any vein: mud mixed with lightning flows through, an unruly fusion of bad blood and good. It's not easy to imagine what would make someone hate a little boy—or, more probably, the parents of that little boy— enough to place not one but two vipers in his cot. *There we were, harmless government administrators, on perfectly good terms with everybody, and all of a sudden some wrong'un came after our only son* doesn't quite ring true to me. Many surmises could be made, and have been made, but when it came right down to it, you had this switchback fanged couple bearing down on a youngster too stunned to even make a sound. Two against one isn't fair. But really it was even simpler than that. The mongoose is the enemy of the serpent. Árpád the First wasn't interested in saving anyone's life. Leaping into that writhing mass and slashing away until it fell still; that's what she was interested in. End of. Or not quite. A third-floor nursery can't really be described as a natural habitat for a mongoose. I almost want to say that someone must have brought her there, but having lived with Árpáds all my life, I know that Árpád the First could just have easily been out looking for trouble and found her own way into that nursery. Basically it's like that song . . . if we don't know by now, we will never, ever, ever, ever know.

Even as a toddler that forebear of mine was the solid type. The mongoose had bolted, but someone had been reading the child potted biographies of wise warriors. One name had got stuck in his head, and he knew it must belong to the mongoose: he waited until he could be heard over the nursery maid's hysterical screams, then he murmured, "Árpád," over and over, with his pudgy little arms outstretched. And once Árpád the First had made herself presentable, she came to see him.

Do Yeon-ssi hadn't heard this legend. There was never the right time or the right sort of atmosphere in which to bring it up. When people ask about Árpád XXX, or about his mother, it's always been simpler just to say, "Yeah, domestic mongooses are the new cats and dogs—it'll catch on, you'll see." But Do Yeon-ssi's lecture on mongoose psychology was far from brief, and I longed to lecture my lecturer, really set the scene for her, give her some idea of . . . I don't know, the intertwining of two fates or something. That was all Montague stuff, though, and I'm a Shin now. I held my peace. Xavier knows all about the Árpáds, but he stayed quiet too. That was no surprise. I've never heard him talk back to his aunt. She's been the parental authority in his life for decades, and he's learned that contradicting her sets up the first link in a chain of counter-contradictions that drags you to the underworld.

Better to immediately cooperate with Do Yeon-ssi . . . that's what Xavier calls her: Miss Do Yeon. Her more old-fashioned friends are shocked that he puts things on a first-name basis like this, but what can Do Yeon-ssi do? She devoutly watched over this brat for so many years, and this is how he repays her . . . by depriving her of the honorifics that are due her. But she's not going to cry over it, that's just the way it goes, she didn't do it for the honorifics anyway . . .

That's how Do Yeon-ssi spins it, with full awareness that Xavier calls her "Miss" in tribute to her heart-shaped petal of a face. Her ink-black hair is streaked with strands of white, and it mostly looks after itself, running semi-divine riot around her shoulders and down her back, making you think of aureoles and oceans. And then there's the look in her eyes. The look of Eve in Eden . . . some amalgam of devotion and brutality that's only really satisfied by encounters with the interior and therefore eviscerates everything in sight. It's fitting for an optical lens magnate to be embodied the way she is, each eye a magnifying glass. I should've known better than to go along with her request to be placed under hypnosis. She asked if I could make it so she'd fall asleep whenever she wanted to. "Deep sleep . . . the kind that gets you really well rested, OK?" She did need more sleep of that kind. After one of her more acute bouts of insomnia, she looks so tired nobody realises she's rich. Those bleary eyes with dark circles around them somehow make everything she's wearing and holding look stolen.

"Yeah, no prob," I said. I was cocky. After all, that was how I made my living at the time. That and boosting diet willpower, deleting fear of public speaking, and some stuff with a few other phobias. My artist friend Spera loves to have a go at me for not putting my "powers" to more profound uses. According to Spera, Emily Dickinson would be disappointed in me. She quotes from Dickinson's letters: *Cherish Power—dear—remember that stands in the Bible between the Kingdom and the Glory, because it is wilder than either of them.* This utterance brought forth the most thoughtful and mature response I could conceive of: sepulchral silence as I dropped a cashew nut down the front of Spera's top. Let others do their bit towards revolutionising human consciousness: I've learned to treat an attention span as a pulse with a regularity observable right down to the millisecond. I make a few test runs, track a few signals, and then I weary my hypnotee into a light stupor with the most minuscule of small talk. With Do Yeon-ssi I picked the issue of daylight savings, listing times I'd been late for appointments because of it, or had been too early, decided to come back later, and then missed the appointment altogether. I also provided meticulous descriptions of the weather on each of the occasions I described, and invited her to share similar experiences. When she declined to do so, I invented daylight savings mix-ups for her, resoundingly minor scenarios I vowed she'd told me about herself. I was loving the way Do Yeon-ssi's face changed as she observed my commitment to the strangely dreary lies I was telling. Her expression had been a mixture of confusion, wonder, and distaste, and it began to congeal into abject dismay. And she kept interjecting to ask when the hypnotism would begin. Ostensibly Do Yeon-ssi was free to tell me to get lost, but she didn't because of the position I occupied. I knew that keeping her captive in that particular way wasn't real power, but it felt close enough. This woman who might not have had the time of day for me under any other circumstances had promised her nephew I'd be just as precious to her as he was. Ha! Xavier would never have talked at her like that, on and on, bulldozing every attempt to change the subject to something that didn't feel like the gory murder of her brain cells. On and on and on, lying in wait at the end of her attention span, stopwatch and tiny scissors in hand, ah, here's my chance, the boredom has become physically unbearable, and then—a gormless chuckle here, a little pressure of the hand there, and had it all gone the way it was supposed to, it would soon have been done; I'd have trimmed the edge off Do Yeon-ssi's sense of time so that she circled and circled the same instant, unable to conceive of any other until the next was presented to her. The energy of such a trance is elemental. At least, that's what I was taught, that the subject is struggling with all their might to break through into the next moment, or to recall the preceding one. And break through they inevitably will, unless— Well, that would depend on the hypnotist's own strength of mind. Us bog-standard Svengalis have about twenty seconds, thirty seconds max, to work with. So we work fast, and our brushstrokes are crude. Into the eerie calm of Do Yeon-ssi's boredom I intended to embed a line of gibberish, a sound pattern she could repeat until it smoothed out into a silken slide that tumbled into a sea of self-undoing. I've overheard Do Yeon-ssi talking to her pillow. All about qualms and grudges and topics to consult Google about in the morning. She recites misremembered poetry stanzas and foreign language phrases she'd never been able to use in ordinary conversation, and then she scolds the pillow for only pretending to understand.

Drifting far from the reach of these day thoughts and night thoughts, Do Yeon-ssi would bag herself a thousand and one nights' worth of sleep over the course of a few hours, I'd prove I was more than just a purveyor of parlour tricks, and Xavier would no longer feel the need to keep track of Do Yeon-ssi's ever-increasing sleeping pill dosage by counting the capsules. And there we'd be: three happy bunnies hopping along together.

Like I said, that was the plan. But I couldn't get a fix on Do Yeon-ssi's attention span at all. I felt her lose interest in our discussion. That happened fairly quickly. But—and here's the horror story—she lost interest without losing focus, continuing to respond to my inanities as if something was actually at stake. It's like this: At a marionette show you find four types of engaged audience—four different philosophies of enjoying the performance. There are those whose attention is reserved solely for the actions of the marionette: that's Árpád XXX, wishing to believe that the figure is alive in one way or another. Then there are the ones who can't and won't stop looking at the puppet master (or seeking signs of the puppet master, if that person is hidden): that's how Xavier is. There are those who watch the faces of their fellow audience members: my preference, obviously, since I'm the one here talking about the other types. And there are those who follow the strings and the strings alone. Do Yeon-ssi is a string watcher. She may not much care about the order of the strings—if they tangle, they tangle. Still, they express something to her, something about the nature of the illusion before her. That's enough of a reason for her to pursue the strings to their vanishing point.

No, Xavier doesn't quarrel with Do Yeon-ssi, and neither do I.

I tuned out as she spoke of Árpád's best interests. I let my thoughts drift across the shabby scholastic heaven that was our aunt's study. Parchment dust, tarnished gilt, faded brocade. Probably hell for an asthmatic, actually. I stuck to unassuming gestures, pouring tea for the three of us and stuffing down the sandwiches and fondant fancies she selected and placed on the edge of my plate. To be fair to Do Yeon-ssi, she made sure I got the most appealing ones every time, occasionally slapping Xavier's hand away when he hindered her objective. She praised Árpád XXX to the skies, yet in the same breath asked us to acknowledge that the dark side of an exceptional mongoose is bound to be exceptionally dark. There was grim talk of overnight deterioration, there were documented cases . . . Do Yeon-ssi read to us from the mid-1960s account of a Bombay mongoose whose latter years were punctuated with inexplicable frenzies . . . this mongoose would completely lose it, for no reason at all, and the only thing that restored her to her right mind was copious Pepsi consumption. I tried not to let it show, but I was a bit shaken by the case of the Bombay mongoose. Not even Coke . . . Pepsi. The preferred beverage of souls damaged beyond repair. I found myself nodding in agreement as Do Yeon-ssi made her closing statements: We three *must* take a trip, Xavier, Árpád, and me. As soon as possible. We'd thank her for it later.

Her first idea had been to buy the train for us. Its backstory struck her as romantic. She showed us an impossibly glossy historical overview one of her secretaries had prepared: centuries ago, when English tea lovers had faced a 119 percent tax on the price of their favourite drink, this train had been a logistical link in a chain forged by tea and emerald smugglers. But these days the train had a permanent resident who wouldn't be parted from her charming home at any price. All Do Yeon-ssi could find out about her was that her name was Ava Kapoor, that the train had belonged to this Ava Kapoor's family from the beginning, and that she was some sort of recluse. Though apparently not the sort who was averse to lovebirds. She seemed young, in spirit, if not in physiology. And she seemed kind. At least that's what I decided after looking at the letter she'd written in response to Do Yeon-ssi's near-harassment. The gist of Ms. Kapoor's reply (puffy little crescent moons drawn above her lowercase *I*'s and *J*'s and all) was that Xavier, Árpád, and I were quite welcome to journey along one of her favourite scenic routes with her, and that she'd drop us off at any train station we wanted, within reason. She wrote of her regret that it might not be possible to meet in person and hoped we wouldn't take that as a snub.

The Lakes and Mountains Route, that's what it said on our ticket, along with our names, the name of the train, and the name of our carriage. That was it. Just imprecise enough to stir my interest: I'd never been on a train that had named carriages instead of numbered ones. Would Ms. Kapoor be driving the train herself so that we four were the only ones on board? I wondered about the route too. Which lakes and mountains? And where? Switzerland? Italy? France? Just how far away could five days of track and tunnel take us?

Xavier said I'd do better to wonder why his nearly eighty-year-old aunt was so keen to get rid of us. The genuine motive was as different from those she'd stated as night is from day—he was very definite about that. Do Yeon-ssi didn't give us a chance to do much pondering either: by the time we thought about digging our suitcases out of our storage room closet, a team of professional packers had already filled the cases with all the essentials, had zipped our gear into diaphanous packing cubes, even. There was Tupperware dotted with minuscule perforations and filled with earthworms, beetles, and just enough air to keep them alive for Árpád's delectation. It felt like Do Yeon-ssi was taking care of everything in advance so she could forget all about us. Right up until then I'd thought she'd found us pleasant and helpful companions, what with all our fetching and carrying and solicitous enquiries. As I thought about it again, Do Yeon-ssi had lived alone on purpose for a long time before Xavier started having nightmares about her slipping in the bath and not being able to call anyone for help. When I tried to see things her way, the credible version went like this: frequent visits from Xavier would've been nice, but sharing her living space with the most attentive nephew ever (and now his partner, and his partner's mongoose) was, perhaps, a bit much. I suppose carers can all too easily become captors, and with the best intentions in the world, we'd become just that.

The train tickets were Do Yeon-ssi's way of asking for a few days off: that's how I put it to Xavier. He admitted that she did deserve at least that much, though he extracted additional promises from her: Yes, she'd take her vitamins every morning without fail. Yes, she'd limit herself to one soju milkshake per day. Yes, she'd immediately ask the nearest bystander for aid with items that would require an inadvisable degree of stooping or stretching to reach by herself. And yes, she'd phone if there was anything, absolutely anything, even very slightly wrong, in which case she could expect us back on her doorstep as soon as we could manage it.

Later, in that pitch-dark train carriage, the very notion of the three of us rushing to Do Yeon-ssi's rescue made me laugh. I mean, locating a light switch was beyond our combined capability, so never mind about achieving anything else.

"OK, there are literally only two sides this thing can be on," I said, after what felt like at least a decade of bumping heads, sharp pokes from fingers and claws, and frankly quite sinister face-licking accompanied by heavy breathing. Darkness seemed to give Árpád (at least I prayed it was Árpád) license to engage in behaviour he wouldn't have in the light. "That's the window, and that side is where we came in. So I'll take this side, and you and Árpád take the other side. Don't rush, and go really small scale . . . Just pat the wall inch by inch . . . No, why have you turned off your flashlight?"

My phone was dead as usual, and Xavier claimed he needed to save the flashlight battery himself. We sought and found a photo of Ava Kapoor so Xavier could confirm that she was who he'd seen, then we settled on the most practical way of finding out what was going on with her: we'd phone her. Xavier texted away, trying to get a phone number for Ava Kapoor from Do Yeon-ssi, and then from Do Yeon-ssi's secretary. Neither replied. I tucked my chin over his shoulder and basked in the glow from his phone screen as he also texted our local stationmaster and made sure she held on to my suitcase until we got back.

"How do you even have her phone number? What . . . the two of you have a whole conversation thread? How far back does this go?"

"Sheila likes train jokes. It's Boughton, Otto. Everyone has everyone else's phone number."

"I don't!"

"Well, you've got that mouthy South London attitude on you, haven't you . . . and remember what a hard time you had falling asleep without the sound of sirens? I have to say, for a while I really wondered if Kent life could ever be for you . . ."

Xavier gave Do Yeon-ssi one more minute to text him back, then he called her on speakerphone. The phone rang for ages before we heard her voicemail greeting. Xavier hung up and rang again. When Do Yeon-ssi answered, she was slurring a bit. Piecing together some of the terminology in noisy background circulation, it soon became clear that she was having a gin rummy party with extra gin. It had been maybe five years since her last gin rummy party, attended by a significant proportion of Europe's hard men and women. So many unsettling things had happened post-festivities (not necessarily the grand cleanup, but the visitors who came over the weeks that followed, complete strangers who kissed Do Yeon-ssi's hands or left the tiniest and stripiest kittens imaginable at her feet and thanked her for "saving their lives") that she'd decided it was probably best not to associate with her gin rummy crowd anymore. But she missed them, I suppose. We had played whist with her whenever we could find a suitable fourth player, but that's a very tame setup if you prefer to play cards for real estate, works of art, or cancellation of others' debt. So out went the whist-playing nephews and in rushed the revellers.

"Anyway, listen, your friend's here with us, so I'm sure you'll get a full report later," said Do Yeon-ssi.

"Which friend?" I asked, and Xavier asked, "One of mine, or one of Otto's?" As if his friends are more virtuous.

We heard Do Yeon-ssi asking if she could finally tell us, then she announced: "It's Yuri!"

"Oh . . . Yuri . . . ," we said, exchanging blank looks.

"I have to say, it's nice having him around. Just . . . easy, you know? Not your usual style at all. I thought you went for angsty types."

Any response Yuri might have been making was swallowed up by what sounded like a full string orchestra playing "I Can't Give You Anything but Love."

I started to tell Do Yeon-ssi I didn't know any Yuri, but a message flashed up on the screen, and Xavier took the phone from me before I had time to read it. All I saw was that it wasn't from a saved contact: the full phone number was displayed. Xavier read the message, then asked: "Er, how did you guys meet?"

Something (or an inebriated someone) crashed to the floor very close to Do Yeon-ssi, there was a hubbub around her, and she said: "What? What? I can't hear you."

"I was asking how you and Yuri met," Xavier said.

"Almost got bathed in hot gumbo from a soup tureen . . . and now you're asking how I met your friend? What do you think is going on? A toy boy and sugar mummy dating service introduced us, something like that? Just keep on thinking that way if you want to . . ."

Xavier glanced at me for confirmation, then said: "It's just that we don't know—"

Another text message arrived. He looked at it and finished, ". . . what we'd do without Yuri."

Clearly he now had some idea who Yuri was. Yet he frowned when Do Yeon-ssi told us the party had been Yuri's idea. To help her unwind. And when it was revealed that she'd asked this very same Yuri about honeymoon ideas and he'd put her in touch with Ava Kapoor, Xavier was livid. "Yeah, he's a nonstop lifestyle guy, Yuri," I said into the phone. "That's what we love about him. Could you put him on for a sec?"

Surprise, surprise: Yuri had been right at her elbow just a second ago, but somebody had whisked him away. What could Do Yeon-ssi say, Yuri was popular. She'd tell him to give us a call: "And don't forget to thank him for the train idea. Right, I've got to go. What did you want again? Ah yes, a phone number. I'll text it to you in—"

Xavier's phone signal flatlined. I left the compartment to check the corridor window: we were going through a tunnel. Once we were out the other side, he followed me into the corridor, switching his handset off and then on again.

"Still no signal?"

"Hang on . . . nope. Lucky for Yuri."

"Our dear, dear friend Yuri. Working tirelessly day and night to guarantee that everyone's relaxed and having fun."

He tapped the corner of his phone against his teeth, thinking.

"That's the thing: it could be genuinely benevolent meddling. Maybe we do owe him a thank-you. But there's something fucked up about having to await outcomes before deciding whether to be nasty or nice."

We'd taken the southeastern-bound train from our station hundreds of times and had thought it'd be the same old route at least until we reached Ashford. Yet here we were puttering along between two heavily weathered stone circles. They were nothing close to Stonehenge height—these circles rose from a field of mud-matted grass that stood almost as tall as they did—in fact they were the height of, well, your average gravestone. No, they *were* gravestones. As we passed we saw that these rings were set concentrically and that they ran deep. "Did you know that we lived this close to something like this?" I asked Xavier. He shook his head, checked his phone screen one more time—still no messages and no signal—then pointed towards the back of the train. "Right, I'll look for Ava that way. See you back here in a bit?"

That meant I was the one who'd approach the driver's carriage. I called out to Árpád, but he'd curled up in the corner of his window seat and had apparently gone to sleep. I put an ear to his snout. Definitely just sleeping. As I straightened up, a patch of the darkness behind me got darker. The sensation was similar to the one you get when someone's staring at you, someone close by but out of your line of sight. I turned around and started to say something, thinking Xavier had come back in. But it was just me and the sleeping mongoose. Xavier had already moved on to the next carriage: I heard him shouting, "Ms. Kapoor? Ms. Kapoor?"

I'd left the compartment door ajar, and now it was closed. I didn't have any specific ideas about this, but I was unhappy with the order in which I'd noticed the changes. The door closes and it gets darker, fine, but it gets darker and then the door closes? No thanks. Thumbs down to whatever mentality I'd boarded this train with, and another thumbs down to this door-and-darkness thing occurring almost as soon as Xavier left me. See—even the term I used . . . left me. Never mind that he had gone to see if somebody needed help—I'd been abandoned! I wasn't sure when and how I'd started thinking like that; I'd have loved to find a way to blame it on the train, but couldn't.

The only thing to do was tackle it all head on. I put a hand to the tinted glass door, pushed, and it didn't open. It didn't open because, I am embarrassed to say, I hadn't actually pushed the door—I'd only thought I had. What-if thoughts had seized me by the wrist and showed me what I expected to happen. I used my other hand and burst out into the corridor, calling out, "Ms. Kapoor," and rapping on the tinted glass of every door on the way to the driver's cabin. I was almost, not quite, running. To make up for lost time. Now that Xavier and I had decided to be gallant, I was feeling competitive about it.

I caught certain personal glimpses of Ava Kapoor as I moved through the next three carriages—these were three of the carriages we hadn't been able to see from the outside. They were arranged to her liking, so the objects and atmosphere spoke of her. The library car was first. Had my phone been in the land of the living I'd have been taking pictures like mad. Since it wasn't, I was more than content to move very slowly and gawp. At the framed photographs of reading rooms in nine libraries across the globe (I recognised two but thought Xavier would probably recognise all of them), at the cubist bookshelves that rippled along the walls like stacked seashells, at the double bed–sized fainting couch upholstered in brocade the colour of Darjeeling tea in the fourth minute of brewing. Cushions in the same shade of copper were scattered across the floor, and books had been left on top of a few of them, bookmarked with pages seemingly torn from other books. If the fainting couch was tea, the mahogany desk was whisky—a great, dark pool of it, with Emeralite lamps for stepping-stones. No visible footprints here, and no Ms. Kapoor, but I had more than half a notion that this tabletop had doubled as her dance floor. Now it was inviting me to dance too. I promised the table I'd be back just after midnight. *Me, you, my earphones, and a top secret tabletop party playlist . . .*

Next came the greenhouse car, where I walked under a green-veined glass roof and alongside a leaf fountain that turned out on closer inspection to be a particularly rowdy lettuce bed. There seemed to have been some sort of accident (or an experiment) with flower seeds: Lettuce battled clusters of violets for space. Summer garlands of tomatoes, peppers, and fat little cucumbers hung from trellised vines, along with a clawed gardening glove or three. I looked out the windows—while there was no sign of the lakes and mountains we'd been promised yet, we were definitely nowhere near Ashford. Just then the train slowed down considerably, as if conceding to give me a clue as to where we were. A few metres away from the track was a pile of earth, or blossoming rock—its peak standing high above the ground, but not quite high enough for it to qualify as a hill. Whatever it was, it was caged in extra spiky barbed wire that seemed to stretch for miles around and above it. The only way this mound could've escaped would have been by drawing itself deeper into the ground until it disappeared from the surface altogether. Though I suppose that would only have served to make its imprisonment more private. Look—I had this heap of earth in front of me, a heap that gave every appearance of having been punished for a wilful act . . . I had to process that somehow. I couldn't tell if we were still in England or not. There weren't any signs. After another second the mound's peak began to bulge in a way that might have alarmed me if I'd been closer. Some sort of accelerated plant growth? A scalding hot mud eruption? As it was, knowing that I only had a few more blinks of the eye to monitor the situation, I switched windows for a better view. It had just been the angle. What I'd seen was a climber arriving at the top of the mound. "What?! What did you do?" I asked. Never mind that my query couldn't be heard or answered—I still had to ask. "What the fuck went wrong in your life that you've ended up where you are?"

The figure stood and threw their head back, seeming to examine the barbed-wire lid that closed them in. Then they limped around the peak and vanished from sight. Stems rustled as I moved to the next window, pulling three baby tomatoes off the nearest vine as I squinted at the mound. The tomatoes were good, only a little sour, so I took three more. The figure on the hill returned to view. Now they were directly facing the train and waving with both hands. I waved back; I couldn't distinguish a single detail of this person's appearance, and don't think they really saw me either. We waved until we were no longer visible to each other in any way. Then I stepped into the next carriage and a barrage of steam that soaked through my clothes and momentarily blinded me besides.

A female-sounding someone insisted I take my shoes off and put them in a basket to my left, so I did. While I was in the middle of that a dressing gown fell on my head and the same someone said I might as well get naked too. It was a sauna we were in, after all. I'd already unbuttoned my shirt before it caught up with me; I was stripping on demand.

"Ms. Kapoor?"

"No."

The carriage was tiled in blue and white and partitioned into gelatinous-looking cubicles with curtain flaps instead of doors. The cubicle walls had a frosted-glass effect so you could see whether or not a cubicle was occupied but were spared particularities. I headed for the only cubicle that held a living form and said: "I'd like to talk to Ms. Kapoor quickly."

"Oh, you would?" the occupant asked, somehow sounding neither hostile nor curious, but quite French. Think Catherine Deneuve circa 1968, her mild amusement as she confronts and dismisses the mysteries of desire with questions like *How could you think even for a second that I was interested in you?* Judging by the shade of skin visible through the glass, it was a black Deneuve I'd just encountered. Black or dark South Asian.

"Yes, I would. You're definitely not Ms. Kapoor?"

The form shifted; she was dabbing her forehead with a towel.

"Well, I wouldn't say 'definitely' not, because things always take some kind of crazy turn when you say 'definitely.' But I'm moderately sure I'm somebody else."

"That person being . . . ?"

"Just another pawn of fate, sweating all my cares away for now. And wondering what's keeping you from doing the same."

I pulled the rest of my clothes off and took a seat in the cubicle behind hers, explaining that it seemed Ms. Kapoor might need help. At the end of a long interval—so long I thought I was going to have to repeat myself—Cubicle Lady asked: "Did she say so herself?" A genuine enquiry this time.

"In a way. We think— I think— We're not . . ." I gave up and asked: "Do *you* think she's OK?"

"Ms. Kapoor is busy," said Cubicle Lady. "Don't bother her."

She told me that I'd want a shower after this, and I'd have to do that in my own carriage. None of which really served as an answer. I took another tack, talking quickly because that information about the showers made it sound as if she was about to leave: "Who else is on board at the moment?"

"What do you mean?"

"You, me, Xavier, Ms. Kapoor, and—?"

Ah . . . A sigh in the near distance, trembling at first, then clear and sure: *Ah* . . .

I jumped to my feet, slipped in my own sweat, banged my head against the cubicle wall, and dropped onto the bench. The sigh lengthened, soared, and swooped, turning to song. I felt my face scrunching up. Not just from the pain from having almost brained myself . . . I was trying to discern what it was I could hear, and the ratio of thrill to fright. Music that makes you shiver in the midst of a sauna . . . what, how, what? The wailer was further away than I'd thought—they'd only felt close at first because it had started up so suddenly and was so distinct from any of the other train sounds. It was further away and . . . not a person. This couldn't even be a recording of a person. Not a wind instrument, not a string instrument. A person after all? It was very, very like a human voice, airily blurring notes with the skill of an operatic coloratura, but the tone was thinner than any oxygen-dependent organism could accomplish without asphyxiating.

"There are just five of us," said Cubicle Lady, paying no attention whatsoever to the sigh-singing. "You, me, Ms. Kapoor, Xavier, and Allegra—she operates the train, though I take over sometimes. A maintenance team will board at the next station, but they'll only be with us for two stops. That's later on this evening. Then tomorrow we'll have the bazaar . . ."

"About this, er, singing," I began to ask.

"I think I know why you asked if there's anybody else," she said.

"Are you not hearing that? That—music?"

The pitch and volume of the singing had increased, the melody doubled (divided? both?) so that I could hardly hear her: "It's an old freight train," she was saying. "No matter what Ms. Kapoor does with it, no matter how she refurbishes and re-refurbishes the interior, it doesn't feel new."

"Oh, well, for whatever it's worth, I like what she's done with it," I said. "But what—"

The song itself was a sweet, soft, cracked little ditty. Milk and cake, a fond caress before the pillow was pressed over your face. Silk caressing your cheek as you were drained of breath . . . you could fight, but you didn't want to.

Cubicle Lady raised her voice: "If you want to help, try not to talk to Ms. Kapoor. Just keep on being a happy twosome and go home with some photos and some good memories."

That did it; the honeymoon advice. One hand to the back of my aching head, I left my own cubicle, put on a dressing gown, and warned: "I'm gonna join you in there."

She pulled her cubicle curtain aside and said, "No need."

The first few things I noticed: She was right about not being Ava Kapoor, she was black, and she looked about the same age as me. Maybe a few years younger, though no more than five, I thought. Her gaze held none of the indifference I'd heard in her voice; the look she gave me was frank and friendly. Her hair had been swept into three different sections and then bundled together so that they ran in a mohawk-like ridge from the base of her temples to the base of her neck. She'd hastily knotted a towel around the upper half of her body when she heard my threat, and her shyness in that respect puzzled me a bit, given that I could very clearly see that she was sitting with her long legs far apart. The distance looked gymnastic—just short of the splits. A floor length (and mostly transparent) waterproof blanket covered those legs, and beneath them was what appeared to be a wooden box.

"Hello."

"Hi."

"Just steaming my parts," she said. "Mugwort keeps them happy."

I folded my arms, unfolded them, folded them again, then gestured in the direction of the singing. "That, next door. Is that . . . Ms. Kapoor?"

The sound stopped the split second I put a name to it. I couldn't help smiling at that.

"It was," Cubicle Lady said, spreading her legs even further. "Hopefully she's finished for the day."

She looked at me. "What's that face about? Ah, you're moved or something."

"You . . . aren't?"

"I hate that racket," she said, with a vehemence that shrank her eyes and puckered her face. But then she caught herself and sent an impish smile my way: "You never exaggerate? Well, good for you."

Realising that I had encountered somebody who had no intention of telling me anything other than practicalities and the planned schedule for our comfort and enjoyment, I began walking backward, all apologies for bothering her and eagerness for the cold shower I was about to have. When she gave a satisfied nod and dropped the curtain. I walked around the back of her cubicle, found a pair of towelling slippers, and put them on, my head throbbing so horribly I momentarily mistook arms for legs and hands for feet. The singing started up again as I stealth-padded towards the door that led to A. Kapoor.

4.

From a short distance the voice had made me shiver in the heat, but up close it only glimmered faintly, like a hook crafted from ice and sunk into the heart. A wound that healed another wound— the pain in my skull swirled away so quickly it left me light-headed. For the second or third time I wondered what Xavier was seeing and hearing right now. What could he possibly have found in the carriages behind ours? Surely it was all happening here.

I was standing in a combined kitchen, dining room, and lounge. This carriage wasn't open plan like the previous ones. It was neat and functional and sensible and felt like a different train altogether. A cheerily coloured one in which every item within reach performed its function and refused to do a single second of overtime. You couldn't ask the chairs to be anything more than a seating option: they were higher up and cleaner than the floor, but that was the offer in its entirety. Beyond the lounge area there were three compartments: one for Cubicle Lady; one for the train driver, Allegra; and Ava Kapoor was in the last one. Her compartment door was closed, so I saw her through the glass—my second seated lady of the day. This one was about the same age as the first but had much better posture. Her glossy black hair bluntly concluded at a point just below her ears, and she was sat on a high stool with some sheet music and what looked like a radio on a stand before her. A radio in combat with the ether, extending antenna-like spears front and sideways. She held her body almost completely still as she leaned towards this walnut-coloured music box; only her hands moved, her wrists gently flexing as she wove air through her fingers. To top it all off, Árpád was splayed across the pillow on the bed behind her, putting his tail to use as a metronome. No, not Árpád—a smaller mongoose, with darker fur, narrower eyes, and rounder ears. The music ebbed and swelled when Ava made a fist, and her lips parted in a smile.

I knocked at the compartment door—harder than I intended to. She looked at me, looked back at her sheet music, and twirled a fraction of a bar of melody around her index finger, then realised what she'd just seen. The theremin lost its celestial tone and squawked like a hoarse parrot as she floundered, then switched it off. The mongoose that wasn't Árpád slid off the bed, skipped across the stream of cables coursing between the theremin and its power source, and circled me, administering a sniff test.

"You," said Ava Kapoor. "What are you doing here?"

"What do people usually say to you after they've heard you play that thing?" I asked. "Do they tell you they're ready to die in your arms?"

She began a smile—a really wonderful one—then, as if remembering that she wasn't supposed to do things like that, she erased it. "What is it? I mean, what d'you want?"

Her vocal tone was warm, and her words very clearly enunciated—think BBC Geordie. She looked behind me. So did the mongoose. I didn't turn, but felt similarly apprehensive. Cubicle Lady wasn't going to stay in the cubicle forever.

"I thought I'd come to see if you're OK. But now I'm seeking permission to die in your arms," I said.

She beckoned me, saying: "Come, then, and see what you get for going around bothering people with your quips." The door between us was still closed, and her fugitive smile broke cover.

"Serious question," I said. "You wrote a word and showed it to Xavier. What did it say?"

"Oh, that . . . it said HELLO. I just knew he was gonna spot me, and I wanted to avoid, well, a meeting like this one. So I tried to get 'hello' out of the way. Is it my turn to ask a serious question now?"

"Ask away."

"Is it true that you once ran into a burning house?"

So Do Yeon-ssi had told her about that. Not such a surprise. Whenever Xavier's aunt introduces me to anyone I have to jump in really quickly and take over before this story comes out. I hardly ever feel like talking about it. But Ava gave me the big-brown-eyes treatment until I explained that it wasn't a whole house, it was just a flat. A distinction she immediately dismissed. For some reason I needed to reduce her impression of my folly. I think about all the time I had to spend hospitalised because of what I did. I think about the damp shadow that spread over me for weeks. Not just damp but thirsty too, that shadow, greedily sucking away at my tear ducts and oesophagus so that I dreaded opening my eyes and retched up half the air I managed to draw in. I think how close to total respiratory failure that fire brought me, how close to brain death. It was folly, all right. And now she was asking why I'd gone in.

"Ms. Shin didn't tell you?"

"She did, but I was hoping you'd speak for yourself."

The mongoose was standing on his hind legs now, eyeing me with even more alertness than Ava was. I gave him a nod. "What's his name?"

"That's Chela. A female. Answer my question."

"I thought there was someone in there. Well. I saw someone. They didn't come out, so I thought . . . obviously the fire brigade was on its way, but . . ."

"You went in and there was no one there."

"I'm told it was a kind of neural blip. The seeing-someone bit, not the acting on it."

"Really? Wouldn't you say that acting on the first blip constitutes a second blip? You know you should have waited for people who'd know what to do. So why didn't you?"

As she asked this, her face took on a glassy, anticipatory look. Hungry for some sort of bleak confession, it seemed. I did what I always do when wary; I played the wag, telling her I'd asked myself what Árpád would do and had acted accordingly.

"Árpád? The mongoose you're travelling with. You're saying you've made him your moral compass?" Disappointed, she turned away, then turned back. "I'm sorry. I mean, he's probably just as dependable as anybody else, if not more. It's just that my own neural blip has been ongoing for years. I suppose I was looking for encouragement."

"I can do encouragement," I said. "What's going on?"

"I'm a member of the Empty Room Club too," she said. "That song I was playing . . . did you really like it? Funny—most don't. Anyway, it was written by a friend of mine. He was a composer. Mostly film scores, but not this song. He . . ."

Ava opened the compartment door, took two quick steps towards me, eyes alight, then held up her hands. It looked as if she was making a note to herself, that she should stop. But she had come closer.

I offered her my arm and asked: "Did he write the song for you?"

She took my arm, and we went on a promenade the length of the carriage and back. The train coursed onto a triple track, then dawdled for a few seconds . . . long enough for two other trains to join us. One on either side. The blinds of the train carriage to the left were drawn closed, but through the windows on our right we could see into a carriage where a nurse in a spotless white uniform leaned over a table, fastidiously cooling a steaming bowl of soup with a folding fan. He stirred the bowl with a thermometer every few seconds, and his billy goat beard wagged with satisfaction each time he checked the temperature. We nodded at him when he looked in our direction, and he nodded back, then closed the window blinds of his carriage too.

"No, the song's called 'For Přemysl at Night,'" Ava said. "Five nights a week for four years, beginning when I was twenty-one . . . I'd go to this tall, thin house in Jesmond Vale, Newcastle—if you saw it, you'd think it was made of enormous marble toothpicks . . ."

"And all the rooms were empty?"

"Ha. Not a bad guess. Actually my friend lived there. Well, we started off as employer and employee. He paid me to visit. My friend Karel . . . he was this gangly fifty-something-year-old with a deeply sulky resting expression; no matter what you said to him, for the first second or two he'd look at you like he was getting told off for something he hadn't even done. But when he smiled it made quite a difference. I'd be like, "Oh my god, you're somewhat appealing, aren't you?!" And he'd go, "I don't know, Ava . . . am I?" I'd get to his house at about a quarter to midnight, and he'd take me to a huge, dark bedroom on the top floor. The floor above his own bedroom. We'd go there, and."

There was no outer change—our arms remained lightly linked, she spoke evenly, her gaze didn't waver—but her pulse had segued into a death-metal drum solo.

"Ava—it's OK. Whatever it is, you can say it."

"It's just that we're getting on and everything, you and me. And now you're gonna think I'm off my head."

"So what if I do? You already think I'm off mine, don't you?"

"Yeah, a bit," she admitted.

"Was he really your friend, this guy? I mean—he didn't do anything unfriendly? Or did he?"

"Who, Karel? No. Allegra worked for him too, and she liked

him, otherwise I wouldn't even have gone there in the first place. You're not gonna hate someone your girlfriend likes, right?"

"Well . . ."

"You've just thought of a trillion exceptions, but that assumption's never failed us yet. Karel would take me to that bedroom, and he'd switch on a nightlight, and he'd give me music he'd composed. One of the songs was the one you heard, 'For Přemysl at Night.' Then he'd go off to sleep in his own room downstairs."

"Leaving you to play to an empty room?"

"Yeah," she said. "Though it did have this sort of lived-in feel to it. Ultra untidy, loads of expensive gear just tossed aside and left in bad condition. The bed looked like it had been properly slept in—the bed linen made all kinds of weird shapes—but it was only blankets and things. I'm afraid of the dark too, so . . ."

"This Karel guy must have been offering you more money than you could refuse."

"He really was. Not that that's saying much. I—we—really needed ready cash. My dad was sick. I really hated leaving him at night; always had it in the back of my mind that this might be our last one . . . Sorry, this isn't what you signed up for. You came for your honeymoon, and here I am blabbing away at you."

"Oh, but we're the Empty Room Club. We have an understanding. I'm hoping your dad got better."

She squeezed my arm. "Thanks for saying so, but he didn't. And he had a lot to say about my night work before he went. He said I shouldn't have taken the job . . . it was an insult not just to my talent but to any musician's. 'Why doesn't this Karel just put a

CD on if music helps him sleep,' he'd say. He scoffed when I tried to tell him it was about having another person there. But I'm glad Karel didn't go down the CD route. A good while later, once we'd become friends, I found out that he'd lost his wife to the same type of cancer my dad was dying of. He had been through some similar things with her. The remissions, the beautiful remissions, then that fucking awful final march. We met a decade after Karel's wife had died . . . He was teetotal, ate healthily, went running every morning, had this schedule that mixed glitzy galas, commercial work, and pet projects, and every now and then he'd suddenly flinch just a tiny bit, for no external reason, and you'd realise he was completely wrecked."

"Flinch?" I said.

"Yeah. He caught himself very, very quickly, but not before I'd seen him huddle up like an arm had been raised against him. Not just any arm—an arm as heavy as a thirty-foot canon, so all he could do was try to come to terms with getting squashed like a raisin. For the first year I didn't think to ask Karel anything about himself, though. All I cared about was funding various end-of-life things for Dad. There were trips we needed to take, and people he needed to see. I had to make it all as painless as possible for him. Dad never asked me for anything; it's just that I had to do that for him. He kept making new friends as we went along . . . said I couldn't expect him to stop enjoying people. He was the greatest exasperation—whew, sorry, one second, please."

She turned her head away, raised her sleeve to her face, looked at me again. "Sorrows of a daddy's girl. He died . . . and I went on playing to the empty room for another three years. Five nights a week, mostly weeknights, overall."

"Jumping at shadows the whole time?"

"It was hard to do at first, let me tell you. Karel would only let me have the nightlight while I was playing, but as soon as he left I'd switch all the lights on and search the room before I started. He'd thump on his bedroom ceiling with a broom handle so I'd get a move on. Anyway . . . after that first night, I was still scared of the dark everywhere except in that empty room, where I played my theremin from midnight to five a.m. And I don't know why."

I scratched my head.

"There's more," she said. "Even though, as I told you, it was an empty room, some of the compositions I played got a better reception than others."

"How could you tell?"

I'd kept my tone neutral, but she raised her chin; her pulse was going again. "I don't know, Otto. That's just how it was. I played some Martinů, some Schillinger, a bit of Fuleihan, some Zappa, and two of Allegra's compositions. He seemed to quite like Allegra's offerings, but it was the song Karel wrote for him that really helped him get some rest."

"Him?"

"Přem. Remember, the song's called 'For Přemysl at Night.' Karel told me I should only ever play it for his son."

"But . . ." Suddenly I thought better of asking.

"Are they dead now, Karel and Přem? Is that what you wanted to ask? Karel is, but I don't know about Přem."

She stopped walking and asked: "Do you?"

"Do I what? Know about Prem?!" I genuinely didn't see how she'd arrived at this question (how and what could I know about this Přemysl of hers?), yet somehow I ended up sounding like a bad liar.

Her eyebrows shot up. I must have smiled first; hers seemed like a reply.

"It's been a peculiar few years. For me, at least, Otto. But it's almost over . . . well, depending on what the doctor says. Oh, hello, Laura."

Cubicle Lady had materialised to my right, fully dressed and exasperated.

"What did I ask you not to do, Mr. Shin?"

"Talk to Ms. Kapoor."

"And what are you doing right at this moment?"

Ava shrugged and gave me a tiny wave, so I said: "Leaving, Laura . . . I'm leaving."

I invited Chela the mongoose along, telling her there was someone she might like to meet. Staring, Laura said: "Sorry, but there's a rule about talking to Chela as well."

Bloody hell. Fine. I went back the way I came without another word.

5.

Xárpád was waiting in our compartment. Xárpád and the continued absence of light.

"You found her?" Xavier asked. He sounded just a little fuzzy; he seemed to have been sitting in there for a while, just staring straight ahead of him.

I took his hand and threaded his fingers through mine. "Yup. It was HELLO, not HELP."

"That's a relief. I'll have to tell her so myself."

"Ah, about that. She does like having us on board and everything, but . . . just in case you see her around . . . we're not actually allowed to talk to her."

"What? Why?"

"Er . . ."

"You didn't find out why."

"It's for health reasons, I reckon. She mentioned a doctor. And seems a bit transfixed by loss. People she knew and loved who are gone."

"Mourning?"

"I don't know if I'd describe it that way. She seems more . . . expectant? Anyway, it's the sort of the thing that takes time, and four days from now we'll be gone. Shouldn't be too difficult to respect her wishes. Just wait 'til you see the library, and taste train-grown tomatoes," I told him. "We can pick violets for our salad too. Maybe even marry Árpád off while we're at it . . ."

"Marry him off to who? Ava Kapoor?!"

"No . . . you'll see. Well, I hope you will."

He slapped his knee. "I'll prepare my share of the bride price accordingly. Also, I see your library and tomatoes and raise you a portrait gallery and a postal-sorting carriage . . ."

Something had disconcerted him as he mentioned those two carriages. Or maybe it was an unconnected thought that crossed his mind; anyway, he let go of my hand. I took a seat opposite him, dumping my jeans, shirt, and Saturday underwear on the neighbouring seat and cautiously tilting backward until my head met the wall, which was unexpectedly plush. I tried to think "velvet cushion" and not "padded cell." Sunlight lined the bottom of the compartment door and the base of the window blinds, but apart from that, the figures of Xavier and Árpád were mainly distinguishable by size and silhouette. One much shorter than me, one taller. One with a tail, one without. Everything mellowed once we sat still, feeling the train in our backs and necks and feet, that affable and determined rattle of the axle within the round, the wheels beneath us carrying us away. I listened intently for a while, for footsteps or some other commotion in the hallway, or the crackling that precedes a tannoy announcement. But there was only quiet. And Árpád's sweet slumber was making me bitter—he could at least have made a show of looking for a power socket or a way to open the window blind. I said as much, and Xavier stretched out his leg and crossed his ankle over one of mine. "It's not too bad like this," he said. "We can talk."

I wiggled my toes. "Can implies ought, Mr. Shin."

"In that case, Mr. Shin, I'll get it all off my chest. I'm thinking about being eleven and twelve," he said.

"Nice and specific . . ."

Veronica Park, Xavier's mum, has saved his first passport, the one he used from the ages of two to twelve. We've looked at it together. Each page is a wall of watermarked squares and rectangles of smudged ink with entry dates and times written in them. Xavier was born during strange times for the Shins of Sangju. This was how Veronica prefaced his childhood situation when I asked her about it. Strange times for the country in general: a towering cream puff of an economic miracle sombrely nibbled away at the edges by martial law. But in addition to that tense prosperity—*only contentment is legal*—there was a lot of pain for the Shins as a clan that just kept shrinking. Infertility, miscarriages, fatal paediatric illness, a terrible accident, cot death— Veronica ticked each vast sorrow off on her fingers and thumb as she told me what her husband's sisters had endured over the course of nine months. And then Veronica gave birth to this sweet-natured little rosebud who bounced with health. He was baptised very quickly and named after the saint who'd converted one of his ancestors to Catholicism. Veronica tried not to like the rosebud too much. He'd hold on to her little finger and give her soulful looks, and she'd stare back, knowing, just knowing, there had to be a catch. By the time he was about four weeks old she was already panic plotting. She'd hide him somewhere. Yes, that's what she'd do, that's how she'd prolong the time they had together. Clownish notions, as if she was Death's jester, thinking up ways to make her laugh by trying to escape her. Veronica and the rosebud stayed exactly where they were, attending all scheduled doctor's appointments as faithfully as they did mass, and, to everyone's surprise, the rosebud made it through his first year without major incident.

Then four of his aunts all but abducted him, squabbling between themselves as they passed him from country to country, each one instructing him to call her Mother, or Mamoune, or Omma. Nobody else in Xavier's family could forget that these four sisters were mothers to children who had only almost been born, or had lived far too briefly. When you thought of that, you knew you didn't have the right or ability to chastise. So Xavier and two of his cousins were dragged around between aunts for years. Do Yeon-ssi, the fifth sister, was the eldest of Xavier's aunts. When she thought about what was going on, she felt weak with fear. It was all wholly ordinary and all utterly out of hand. She'd been keeping an eye on Xavier and surreptitiously comparing him to her friends' twelve-year-old kids. He was all worn out from being given different names and not knowing what to call people or how much affection to show, or whether to bother saying anything at all to anyone since he didn't know how long it would be before the next sister swooped in. Thinking about all this, Do Yeon-ssi had a talk with Veronica Park. She pointed out that her home was Xavier's best chance of a stable environment. She's a person whose sisters don't love her but fear her, because of all the things she did to guarantee that when they were all growing up. This must be true, since the house of Shin Do Yeon turned out to be the only place Xavier's other aunts didn't dare try to take him from.

"Eleven and twelve," Xavier said. "Those were the years when I was spending a lot of time in compartments like this. Only with people I didn't know, or just me and a book. It mostly felt safe, but also, how do I put this . . ."

"Like some kind of incubator for intense encounters?"

"Yes! Even more than stations are. Is it that sticky mix of enclosure and exposure? The temporary privacy? You just get . . . involved with each other. Can't avoid it."

"And where was that? São Paulo?"

"Nope, São Paulo was the year before, I think. This was the route between Paris and Marseilles. By the way, are you completely naked underneath that dressing gown?"

"You're too easily distracted. And you're getting nothing from me until you tell all about this French train orgy."

"Did you see that?" he asked.

"What?"

"I just rolled my eyes. Good, you didn't see it. So if you do it too, I won't know. This is perfect."

When Xavier Shin was eleven years old, the Parisian couple he lived with at the time sent him to boarding school in Provence. They had driven him there and back at the beginning and end of the first few terms, but midway through his second year, partly because both of them liked a drink too much to volunteer as designated driver, they suggested taking the train instead. The journey by train was almost four hours long, and he travelled unaccompanied. That didn't seem appropriate for a child as soft-spoken and baby-faced as he was, but all he really had to do was find the right platform at Gare de Lyon or at Gare de Marseille St. Charles, sit on the train, and be met on the other side by a responsible adult. Other passengers looked out for him, thinking him neglected or lost, but he was fine. He read comic books, began and completed homework assignments, or he listened to Handel's water music on his Walkman, imagining that it had been composed for him to listen to aboard a flower-bedecked barge on the river Thames. All of this was more than preferable to the train ride Xavier had taken with a pair of inordinately squiffy parental bodies who'd lugged him from car to car inviting other passengers to quiz him on his weakest academic subjects . . . *That will teach you, Francis Xavier Jae Kyung Shin . . . that will teach you to get a B in History.* Oh, and just like a radioactive rainbow following acid rain, Mamoune's star turn: accusing a frail old lady of stealing her pearl necklace, snatching the pearls off the lady's neck, then realising, when she put it on and strand clinked against strand, that she was already wearing the necklace she'd been thinking of. After that Xavier took the train unaccompanied, or he didn't go at all. That was the ultimatum he made, and they could tell he was serious.

One July afternoon, he was on his way back to those Paris people for the summer, body in his seat, mind hopping backward along the track, gaze holographically layering the chalky ridges that outlined miles and miles of storage crates over the bucolic picture-postcard scenes the windows had shown him just a few minutes ago. He was thinking, *Six weeks, six whole weeks.* He was at an age where six weeks made the difference between one shoe size and another. He was getting taller and broader and all the rest of it . . . by autumn he'd practically be somebody else. Body-wise, anyway. Yet he'd still be stuck with the same parental bodies, the ones who'd arranged a best friend and auxiliary friends for him. The best friend and the auxiliary friends were no more interested in Xavier than Xavier was in them, but none of them could escape the unfortunate fate of being the offspring of business associates. On summer afternoons they roamed the grounds of Disneyland Paris, the Palace of Versailles, or the Jardin du Luxembourg, each member of the group lost in silent and unsmiling thought, the ones who had real friends keeping an eye on their watches so they could dash off as soon as this chore was over. The group was international in appearance and dressed in varying shades of a colour that had been agreed upon the night before, so they looked like a meditative gang or the junior branch of a cult. Other children would approach in twos and threes and shyly ask if they could join. These were the pastimes that would eat up Xavier's summer weeks, then a few days before he was due to go back to school, his "what I did over the summer" essay would be dictated to him, with the aid of exhibition catalogs from various galleries the Paris parents had visited by themselves. It had been explained that it wasn't really lying for Xavier to say that he'd gone along to the galleries too, because that definitely would have happened, if not for the fact that mixed in with the masterworks there were many sights that would be detrimental to his moral and emotional development. Xavier guessed that this year he would write that he had been to the Uffizi, the Kunsthistorisches Museum, and the Rijksmuseum, and that he would claim he saw paintings of bread, cheese, apples, vases of flowers, and holy families, just like the ones he said he'd seen at the Courtauld Gallery and Sternberg Palace. He'd write the essay without looking at the pages of the book proffered to him: "This one, see?" He didn't care for paintings of bread, cheese, apples, vases of flowers, and holy families . . . they made him want to go out and join a crime syndicate. A much less refined gang than the one he was certain the Paris parents were part of. Yet Xavier Shin would take the dictation without changing a word, shaking his head as he did so. Xavier was the type of kid who scored highly in nonverbal reasoning tests. It was too soon for him to claim to know much about life, but he could tell this wasn't it. Thinking about the six weeks ahead of him, the schoolboy got all jittery about the legs. He was alone in the compartment, so he didn't have to make a pretence of composure; he could hunch up, hug his kneecaps, and say, *Stop it, stop it.* But it continued, bone bashing bone, as if his left leg was hell-bent on pulverising his right, and vice versa.

Xavier told his knees that the people he was living with weren't that bad. There was that last-minute summer trip he'd taken with the male Paris parent—Xavier had had to go with him because the female Paris parent was away and there was no time to arrange to leave him with anyone. The male Paris parent had received a phone call very early in the morning. He hadn't said much, only held the phone away from his ear and grimaced as high-decibel howls of hysteria interspersed with heavily accented French ricocheted around the room. A couple of hours later, Xavier and the male Paris parent were on their way to Macao, where they'd taken gondola ride after gondola ride, drifting between the artfully begrimed pillars of a casino's underground fantasy of Venice. The blue of their gondola was even brighter than the LED sky above, and there were these pastries . . . little clouds of flaky, butter-fattened flour crowned with silken custard. At some point during the course of these meetings—for it was meetings Xavier's companion was conducting in these gondolas, the male Paris parent and some third passenger writing out figures on their respective notepads, then either nodding or reaching out to cross out a figure and replace it with a new one more to their liking—the male Paris parent said to Xavier: "This Venice is better than Venice Venice, you know. You have a better time when you're not expecting anything real. That's why seriously tacky people manage to enjoy themselves wherever they are."

There was nothing about the view from their gondola that he didn't like, so that was how Xavier Shin discovered he was a seriously tacky person. You could wander around Venice Venice during the day, and you could do the same thing at night, but you got more bang for your buck here, because in this cavernous basement it was both day and night. You could see it in the way they were acting, the lovers and the shoppers and the selfie takers and the cocktail-supping bon vivants strolling unhurriedly around this little campo; it was whatever time they wanted it to be. As for the houses that lined the square—they had twice as much personality as they would've had if they'd had to choose between a.m.

and p.m. The daylight gave the stone facades a feathered glow, and crackles of light from the streetlamps painted thick zigzags of shade over and under the eaves. The combination made the houses look . . . loud. They seemed inhabited by spirits too high to be contained. You could even fancy that the barcarolles roving across the water originated with the houses, and not some discordant choir of invisible gondoliers (or speakers emitting a looped soundtrack). Xavier wouldn't really have minded visiting more imitation cities. Disneyland wasn't the same. There was no amazing aftertaste of citrus-sharp malice after trips to Disneyland, no sense of irreality pouncing upon the real and quite deliberately eating it for breakfast. But the day at the Venetian Macao was a one-off, and he wasn't allowed to tell anyone about it. Not truthfully, anyway. The official story was that they'd been to Venice Venice. Par for the course, really.

The Paris parents overwhelmed him with their secrecy. Some of it was absolutely necessary in terms of avoiding prison, but there were too many non-illegal matters that they did their utmost to cover up. Things like having vulgar tastes, or not being happy, or being stressed out. He knew that sooner or later they would make him just like them, hiding things instead of dealing with them. Through the window he watched grass turn to water, water to concrete, concrete to scrawny trees, then hedgerows, leaf to stone, then back again, the landscape clothing itself in uninspired uniforms of grey, brown, black, and blue as it jogged alongside the train, no longer expanding the horizon but levelling it. It was as if a great rusty zip was closing in all his senses. Two pairs

of police officers boarded the train at Avignon station, blue padded vests and all. A sight rare enough to make him consider not
sitting like someone who was possibly hiding something. But they
passed his compartment door without saying anything. Clearly
they had much bigger fish to fry. Xavier was in the fifth of ten
carriages, and he heard four pairs of feet part ways at the furthest
door. Two pairs went onward, and two returned, went further
back. He kept his head down and stayed as he was for maybe
seven stops, legs gathered up against his chest, peering out from
under his elbow as the station names changed. Pressing his fingers and thumbs to his patellas had a soothing effect, as if his
fingerprints were unlocking the rest of him. Someone wheeling
a refreshment cart down the corridor stopped to tell Xavier he
seemed dehydrated, and was ignored. "Look, you don't have to
buy a drink, but why sit here alone?" said the vendor. "I don't
know if you saw, but there are police on board, looking for someone. Join the family next door, OK? Don't give some escaped con-
vict a chance to come in here and cause problems . . ."

Xavier said, "OK, thanks, I'll move," but he didn't. A cold,
slick veil fell between him and all the figures he saw, all the post-
ers advertising films and foodstuffs. Everything swirled and then
separated into droplets of oil and sweat. The train stopped and
started up again, two passengers breezed into the compartment
and took seats facing each other, but he didn't look up or loosen
his grip on his knees. The police officers were still on the train—
at least that's what these newcomers were saying, and he didn't
think escaped convicts could wonder aloud about *les flics* with

quite as unconcerned an air as these two. One of them sounded like a girlish Québécois, and the other voice, much deeper, spoke with an accent that was harder to place. The conductor popped in to check their tickets, and when he'd left, the male voice addressed Xavier in a gruff and grandfatherly way: "Young man, are you in pain? Is there anything we can do for you?"

The directness of the question—"Are you in pain?" replacing more typical formulations like "Are you all right?" or "Hope nothing's wrong?" almost led Xavier to confess, but after a beat the girlish voice piped up. He guessed she was a couple of years older than him, if that. "Let's not bother him, Papa. He's a thinker, thinking . . ."

"She's right," Xavier said into his trousers. "That's what I'm doing. But thank you for asking; please enjoy your journey."

The girl's delighted "Ha" sparked a haphazard wish for an older sister, someone at home who talked to and about him like this, mocking and affectionate in equal measure. She'd drive everyone completely mad with her cynically idealistic remarks as they grew up—friends, other family members, would be suitors, colleagues, everyone—and he, Xavier Shin, would be her most partisan associate. This sister of his would always be able to say, "Well, Xavier knows what I mean!" even if he didn't. He listened as the other two arranged their board and discussed the order of play, the grandfatherly sounding father good humouredly fending off accusations of having plotted his own defeat in advance. Hearing them like each other aloud was almost as bad as the leg spasms. He drew such comfort from their company, from their existence, that he almost wished they'd leave. It had been better before they came. Before they'd swanned in, he had almost coaxed himself into thinking that this was what the train home was like for most people, and there was no good reason why things should be different for him. Most people feel themselves depart as they arrive at their station. We'd all like to keep the impressions we just gathered, keep the hope we had and the interest we took in our surroundings; we'd like to be like that all the time and every day, but by the time you get home, that's all snuffed out. In you go, in you go, creature who dwells in the stationery box, in you go, clutching your withered posy . . .

Xavier had a hunch that these two were somehow exempt. How had they managed it? They played their board game, and against the backdrop of sound they made (muffled exclamations, drawn out "hmms," pebbles knocking wood), Xavier heard the name of his station announced. He watched and listened as passengers boarded and disembarked. And as the train swept onward he also glimpsed the male Paris parent standing near the ticket barrier in animated conversation with a station guard, possibly being told a son wasn't something you could ask about at the Lost Property counter. He emptied his lungs all the way out, then fully restocked. What did he do now that he'd missed his stop and his treacherous legs had very conveniently gone back to normal? Think, he had to think. There was every chance that his two carriage-mates would get off at the very next station, but he wished so much that they would stay awhile. Not for long. Just for, say, three more stops. Then he'd turn around and face the six weeks.

He dropped his feet onto the floor, raised his arms, rolled his neck around a few times to get the crick out of it, looked at the grandfatherly father and then at the girl. A stocky black man with a button nose and so many smile lines his entire mouth area looked crumpled. His daughter resembled him about the nose but had otherwise branched out on her own with a patron-saint-of-adventuresses look. Twinkly eyes, masses of frank forehead, and a halo of curls. They were playing Baduk. The girl's hand hovered above the square she'd just chosen, and Xavier could see why she'd been cross in advance about her dad letting her win. She'd probably thought she was a Baduk genius, had never lost a game since birth . . . until she'd faced an opponent other than this man, who was mysteriously and embarrassingly bad at Baduk. Both father and daughter were older than he'd expected. The girl looked about sixteen, and the man about sixty. Xavier didn't seem to look the way they'd thought he would either—he supposed he seemed younger. The surprise wasn't unpleasant on either side, though the girl did raise her eyebrows and ask if Xavier was a runaway or what.

Which led him to consider what exactly he was. He came to some conclusions he couldn't share. His mouth couldn't say that he'd been given one shell to inhabit, only one—the obedient son of the Paris parents. And now that he'd passed the station where the male Paris parent was waiting for him, that shell was in pieces, and he'd fallen out, neither solid nor liquid, but a wisp of air, easily dispersed. Doubtless they'd already begun—phone calls, messages, arrangements: "Yes, same as last time." The Paris parents had had other sons, boys from other branches of his family they'd taken guardianship of with promises to turn them into cultured and highly educated men. Disappointments one and all. So now, again, the things in the son's room would be given away, his with-drawal from school records would be made in absentia, and any-body who'd ever had anything to do with him would be made aware that he'd been sent abroad. To a better school, or for treat-ment, because his health had taken a very serious downturn. Even if he went back to them now, one or the other of them would be on the way to Switzerland or somewhere, passport in hand, more than capable of looking him quite calmly in the face and saying, "This is very sad, and I do hope you find your own parents, but my son is very sick, my partner is with him right now, I'm just on my way to visit them." He had deliberately missed his stop, and that was how he'd become a secret, to be walled up in darkness along with all the other matters the Paris parents couldn't let any-body know about. Xavier was so frightened he was sure his heart would implode, but he smiled at the girl and her father. He was thinking: *Even if this is it for me, I'll be smiling as I go. I want the Paris parents to find out about it and wonder what that crazy little bastard was smiling about as he died . . . and as they ask themselves about that I want them to feel like something's coming for them . . .*

Xavier told them he was on a trip with his mother. And if you want to make a list of things that are scary, put words at the top. Because just as the girl and her father had begun to gently dis-mantle Xavier's assertion—his mother had been gone for quite a while, hadn't she, where were her things, and so on—a woman who could very easily pass as Xavier's mother stepped into the compartment and sat down with them. Age, check; face just as Korean as his was, check; soft drink brought back from the restaurant car for her patiently waiting son, check. Two drinks, actually. One for him and one for the girl, whose name he still didn't know.

"Oof, such a queue . . . ," the woman said. Her soft, raspy accent was familiar to him—it was from Burgundy, just like his favourite French teacher, who always sounded as if he was talking through a mouthful of sugar cubes. But the accent was the only thing Xavier recognised. Everything else about the woman was like a warning not to lie, never, ever to lie unless you wanted what you said to come true. She was wearing an SNCF uniform, navy and red, but she whirled her loose hair up into a bun, pulled a gauzy white shawl out of a leather tote, and draped it around her shoulders as she took her seat beside the girl Xavier had imagined was his sibling. The newcomer proceeded to slap a can of Ricqlès down in front of each of the two youngest passengers, who now found themselves facing each other with identical wide-eyed stares, as if perhaps this being who'd gone from SNCF employee to archetype of chic maternity in two seconds flat could still be banished if only they didn't make eye contact with her. They sought out the emergency cord instead. Xavier couldn't see it, so he had to assume the girl had her eyes fixed on it. It was high up and to the right of his head, far from the window. Quite a scramble, even if you could count on not being tackled before you got there.

"Draw the curtains and drink up, kids," the woman said, gesturing with something pearl grey that seemed to fold over and under the lines of her hand—a gauntlet? Xavier glanced at it: it was an exceedingly ladylike pistol. The girl's father, who had actually been looking at the woman, had caught this development in real time. No wonder he'd kept his reaction minimal. The girl arranged the curtains from her side, and Xavier mirrored her actions. Xavier opened his can of minty fizz, and so did the girl. Now looking anywhere but at each other, they drank up, somehow managing not to choke. The woman turned the pistol on the girl's father, who rubbed his face hard and in slow motion, trying to wake himself up. *At the count of ten . . .*

"You're going to shoot me? Why?"

The man looked at the woman as he asked this, and the question was posed in English. The woman took a pair of handcuffs from her tote and threw them over to Xavier, who caught them reflexively, though he fumbled with the keys she threw half a second later. "Cuff his ankles," she instructed in French, then tapped her gun against the tabletop. "Quickly. Now."

Kneeling on the carriage floor, flinching in expectation of kicks to the face administered either by the man or his daughter, Xavier mumbled apologies as he snapped the cuffs around silk-clad ankles. He rose, slid the keys across the table to this newly materialised mother of his, and she jangled them in the man's direction and addressed him in French: "No running off, sir. We're about to play Go."

Still in English, the man said, "The police will pass by soon. They'll see this. Is that OK with you?"

The woman looked down at the Baduk board and then swept the grid clean with one hand, sending stones shooting in every direction. The man put his hand on Xavier's arm, asking in English: "Young man, do you understand me?"

Xavier nodded.

"But *she* doesn't, right?"

Xavier looked across the table at the woman who so urgently wanted to play Go that she was prepared to play it under these conditions, with an ankle-cuffed opponent and a pistol in one hand. She had liquid labyrinths for eyes, and the more the man spoke English to her and to Xavier, the more likely it began to seem that she was going to shoot them all. It was very, very difficult to tell if this was language-barrier frustration or a more general irritability. Xavier avoided taking linguistic sides by shrugging.

"Can you tell her," the man said. "Can you tell her that even though she would rather talk in French, I can't right now. I was never fluent in the first place, and right now—it's all gone. I'm pissing myself here. Because of my daughter . . . just ask her to let my daughter go first. Fuck. The girl never wanted to take this trip anyway. Who cares about that bar in Montmartre where the pianist has his newspaper set up in front of him in place of a music score and all the regulars know to leave the street door open so the breeze can turn the pages for him; you'd better just care about that sort of thing on your own, that's what my daughter says. Let's send Laura away first; then we can talk any way she wants."

Xavier could have squeaked, *And what about me?* But saved his breath. The girl didn't say anything either, though it was clear that if she was going to pick a battle, it would be the one against any heroics her dad tried to pull.

"He seems upset," the woman said to Xavier. "What did he just say?"

The boy hesitated. He wasn't so sure that she didn't already understand. But he couldn't think of a reason for her to test him like this. Then again, he couldn't think of a reason for anything she'd done so far.

He'd wavered too long: the man's daughter answered for him. "He wants to know why you're doing this," the girl said, and then came the uncanny quiet of the minute or two that followed, the little coughing sounds she made as the woman pistol-whipped her, the flailing of her hands. She sank down into the corner of her seat, her face turned to the wall, her breathing shallow but regular.

Having made her point, the woman turned to Xavier and asked again. "What did he say?"

Xavier was quick with his answer this time: "Right now he's saying please, please."

"And before?"

Xavier told her, hoping panic hadn't altered his memory. The woman took a sip of Xavier's drink as she listened, and then she said: "Well, yes. That can happen to the best of us: going blank at moments when it's really important to get things right. Good thing you're here."

She told Xavier to pick up the Baduk stones and put the black stones on her side and the white stones on the man's side. She talked as he did so, telling the man they were going to play until the last stop. The man nodded, his gaze flitting from his daughter to the window to the compartment door . . . How was he going to play Baduk with his pupils sliding in and out of focus like that . . .

The man was saying: "Why isn't anybody coming? Oh God, what has this woman done . . . Why isn't anybody even passing by?" The man's daughter stirred, and the man kept his eyes on her from then on, his tone softening as he spoke to her; Xavier didn't understand what he was saying, but it sounded as if he was trying to keep her as alert as possible, asking her to keep her eyes open, something like that. "Laura . . . Laurinha . . ." Whatever it was the man had said, it served to rouse the girl somewhat; she answered him in French, muttering that he should clear his mind and just play. She told him to make sure to win and that she was cheering him on. "Proud of you, Dad . . ." She seemed to have decided that they were at a tournament. She agreed to keep her eyes open a little while longer.

Xavier watched the woman with apprehension; she'd grown misty-eyed, and it couldn't be the case that she was touched by her own handiwork. She sighed, leaned forward, and told Xavier he was sitting next to a brilliant man.

OK, he was sitting next to a brilliant man, and she was sitting beside a barely conscious girl who was leaking blood from her left ear. As for why nobody had come . . . Xavier very clearly pictured every passenger in the carriages on either side slumped in their seats—it wouldn't have been free goodies offered from the refreshment cart that would've sent them to dreamland. People can be so picky and you can't always rely on them to accept free food or drink, so she'd probably secreted some kind of canister above the back wheels of the cart and trundled through those carriages with a heady haze in her wake, not thick enough to cause wheezing but conspicuous enough to cause complaints about not being able to open the windows before everybody nodded off. Xavier didn't know what he and this woman really had to do with each other, but he felt like he'd been cursed with an ability to read only one mind: the one he least wished to.

"A brilliant man," the woman repeated. "Duarte De Souza."

The man mumbled, "Call me Eddy . . ."

The woman paused to glare at him, then continued: "He was North American Go champion for seven years in a row. And, you know, eligibility is on a geographical basis, not a cultural one. So you've got the cream of America and Canada's considerable crop, you've also got contestants from twenty-one other countries, and you've also got contenders from eleven independent territories and I can't remember how many islands. But Monsieur De Souza sent them all packing for seven years! People started saying the things they've always said about virtuosity. They'd say he had a pact with the devil, or that he was a robot . . . Actually, some engineers started building a robot of their own, to see if it could learn enough about the game to beat him, but he retired before they could finish."

"Ah," said Xavier. North American Go champion. Could such a person actually exist? She might as well have said the man sat beside him was Fantômas—that seemed more likely. Xavier looked at Eddy, to see if he'd understood the woman. He had, and he said: "That's a very selective view. She neglects to mention that once a North American Go champion tries to compete internationally, forget about it. I was never able to clear the preliminary round for the LG Cup. She should pick on someone else."

The woman listened with knitted brow, then turned to Xavier with an enquiring expression.

"He says . . ." Xavier took a deep breath, today was lies-come-true day, plus he thought he could guess what she wanted to hear. "He says he remembers you. You play to an international standard, not just regional, that's what he said. You're LG Cup standard." Surely a little flattery couldn't hurt?

The woman reached for Xavier's can of Ricqlès, then changed her mind mid-reach. There could be no toilet breaks, so she had to pace herself. She began to count the Baduk stones on her side of the board instead. Without looking up, she said: "Hmmm . . . he's lying about remembering me. I don't look like I did back then. The prison years show."

The bit about prison seemed to ring a bell and earned her a piercing glance from Eddy, then a much longer second look. He nudged Xavier. "This person . . . this person already beat me," he said. "It was my second-to-last championship tournament, and she broke my eight-year winning streak. She was magnificent. I can't believe it's her . . ."

What . . . they really had met before? Plus, Xavier had had to leave a bit out. Eddy's words of awed approval included something along the lines of "this person wrecked my strategy like a quickly scattering pair of evil bitch demon pincers." Which exceeded Xavier's own French vocabulary limit. *He says your strategy was . . . like a force of a nature?* Nah. The part of him that would grow up to be a ghostwriter was already evaluating how convincingly he could pass his own voice off as someone else's.

She wasn't the type who slowed down for compliments anyway. "If you remember that much, sir, then you must remember all the letters I wrote to you afterwards," she said.

"Letters?" said Eddy (in English), and then Xavier (in French).

"You never replied. Perhaps you never read past the part where I demanded a rematch. Mere formalities: I didn't really have any hope that you'd agree to that of your own free will. But I do want to know—" The woman had finished counting the black stones and stretched a hand across the board to count the white stones. "Did you truly play your best that day?"

Eddy and Xavier babbled in duet: Of course Eddy had been playing his best. The game became a matter of not losing, of not being humiliated in front of the crowd of spectators who'd come to see Eddy De Souza beat a young upstart nobody had even heard of before this tournament. He'd drawn on every resource he had in order to withstand her aggression. And he'd still lost.

"A weed, your fans were calling me. And you were the mighty pesticide. Some people came up to you backstage wearing 'Mighty Pesticide' T-shirts—"

"Do you think I liked any of that?" (Eddy's English words were faithfully echoed in French, though Xavier took care to point at Eddy when he said "I" . . .)

"You signed their T-shirts, Monsieur De Souza. So I don't know what to think. But that doesn't matter. I could hardly say anything about T-shirts when I was wearing my own floral-print monstrosity with the logo of a soap company and 'WASH YOUR HANDS BEFORE YOU *GO*' printed on the front and back. I'd had to talk a local manufacturer into sponsoring me; there was no other way I'd have been able to fly to Mexico City for the final. And I had to play you. There are more skilled technicians than you, but you're the lyric poet of this game. You saved me without

knowing it. I'd just lost my job at a stationery company in Gatin-
eau. But things like that are hardly rare, are they. I'd been promised promotions and a pension and all the rest of it, and then one
of my superiors messed up some figures. Perhaps with criminal
intent, but more probably out of laziness, I think, knowing that
guy. I wasn't quick enough to get out of the way when he turned
around to point the finger. And I was clueless right up until the
final meeting with Human Resources. I asked about my cardboard box. You always see it on TV and at the cinema—the employee walking away from their desk with the cardboard box full
of personal effects. And the gentleman at HR said, 'Look, if you
want a box, we'll sell you one for fourteen dollars, but don't you
already have some plastic bags somewhere, you could just use
those.' Oh yes, I could have taken the company to court, gone
bankrupt, and probably still lost the case . . . Instead I took my
severance pay and left with my plastic bags, completely demor-
alised. I didn't even have the heart to try to change what was on
record about my dismissal. That I was an untrustworthy employee and so on. I did temp work when I could get it, and I read
the papers . . . There was an article about you. The photo of you
was just a photo, the face of a winner, so what? But there was
another picture, of the board at the end of the game you'd just
won. You'd played white. Night had fallen all across the board,
but you'd exploded stars all the way across it and even brought the
moon crashing down right in the middle. Stars, moon, that's not
really what I mean, but . . . I saw it when I closed my eyes. I can
still reproduce the pattern stone for stone right now. But seeing it
all develop . . . that's different, better. Watching your games made

me feel as if I could begin again. Even as I placed the losing stones, I shared in the making of the art. So I was fine just playing until I won enough games for it to be clear that this wasn't just love of the game—there was aptitude too. Then I got greedy. It was a three-year project, competing until I qualified for the tournament, then working my way up the ranking so I could play you. All I studied were the kingdoms you laid out on the board. Your orthodoxies, your breaks with convention, your gambits. And the funny thing is, knowing those inside and out were almost enough for me to beat my other opponents. I did have to tamper with the schedule a bit, eliminate a couple of people I knew I couldn't beat so I'd be assigned new opponents with less intimidating game history. But it was all arranged so that I wouldn't be found out until after the final, and I was willing to do the time. I don't know that I even wanted to beat you, sir. I just wanted that game. Every fifth or sixth move a meteor flight . . . Ah, this moon-and-stars talk again. That's what you lyric poets do to us. You reveal the indescribable, and then we go gaga."

The woman's gun hand held steady throughout, monitoring the girl beside her, whose inactivity she was probably wise to mistrust, before travelling around to Eddy and then back to the girl again. It seemed she thought of Xavier as a teammate now; no looking down the barrel of her pistol for him.

The train stopped at a station. A silent station, and no one boarded.

Eddy De Souza said (and Xavier translated): "Madame Hébert—that's your name, isn't it, Louise Hébert? I swear to you that I played to the best of my ability that day. And if we played now . . . fright aside, I would be at my worst. I don't think about Go for thirty minutes out of every hour the way I used to. My moves are flabby; they've had no exercise in years. You've already won. You know that."

"Yes, yes—in front of an audience that didn't move or make a sound when my win was confirmed. I remember looking around as the lights beyond the stage came up, expecting to see all the seats empty, since it was so quiet. But they were all there, glaring. There was a little motion here and there as some people shook their heads . . ."

"I lost even though I had their support, Madame Hébert. And you won without it. What, then, do you need from those people? You say you came just to play me. Did you forget that I stood up and applauded you? With sincere respect . . ."

"And when nobody joined you, it started to look like sarcasm. It was so strange, a few minutes later, struggling to hold up the trophy so a photograph could be taken. I'd gained nothing. In fact, I'd been depleted. It felt like my arms would shatter or something. But I was careful to follow the instructions I'd been given beforehand. In the event of a win, I had to hold the trophy up high so the T-shirt was clearly visible and anyone looking for some small way to partake in the glory would know which brand of soap they should wash their hands with before they Go. The photographer took one quick snap and left . . ."

The woman was directing all her answers at Xavier, since all the replies she understood came from him. Light flared through the curtain, and the carriage clattered as it burst out into the sunshine again. The next stop was the last, and it felt as if the driver was picking up speed, intent on the final dash.

"Madame Hébert—"

"And then every account of the match added that you hadn't been in top condition, do you remember that? Your hands had been trembling earlier on, or you had a cold, or something."

"I don't know why anybody would think that. It wasn't anything I said. If anybody had asked me, I'd have assured them that I wasn't at any disadvantage. Madame Hébert, I think people were just . . ."

Eddy thought for a moment, then asked Xavier for some paper and a pen. Upon receipt of both, he wrote a simple declaration to the effect that he, Duarte De Souza, had been defeated by Louise Hébert, superbly and in all fairness, on such and such a date in Mexico City, and that the title of North American Go Champion for that year was rightfully hers. He signed the note and handed it to her. But he had written it in English, and when Louise Hébert saw that, tears ran down her face. She said: "I don't know what this says. I'm sorry. I shouldn't have scared you so badly."

Xavier indicated that he would read it to her. But she, Louise, the woman with the dove grey pistol, the person whose mind Xavier couldn't read after all, said: "Time to take my medicine." She took a small bottle out of her handbag, sprayed some of its contents down her throat, gargled for a second, then tipped her head back and began swallowing Baduk stones exactly as if they were pills.

Things got hazy for Xavier after that. He understood a bit

more when he visited the first arrondissement commissariat that evening. One or the other of the Paris parents had called Do Yeon-ssi—they'd had no plans to let him disappear without a trace, had in fact been panic struck when he hadn't appeared at Gare de Lyon—and Xavier sat hand in hand with his aunt as they watched some footage from the train. He hadn't been able to see any of the onboard cameras, but they were of course right there recording, though the footage could only be viewed remotely and with a time delay. The security guard who had been watching had been quite tentative about raising the alarm at first. The sleeping passengers in the carriages on either side of the Go carriage hadn't fallen asleep instantaneously, or even en masse. It had happened a couple of stops after the police had disembarked, and it had all looked natural enough. One passenger settling down to sleep, the sight of which reminded another passenger that they too could do with a nap. It happens. Just like with yawning . . . someone yawns and then you have to as well, you just have to, even if you're not tired. The woman-with-a-gun-swallowing-stones situation was much less ambiguous, though nobody was quite sure how to proceed regarding the girl Hébert had assaulted. Laura De Souza. Laura, who'd snatched up the pistol, pressed it against Louise Hébert's forehead, and eventually managed to pull the trigger after a lot of fumbling. The woman's patience while the girl worked out how to fire should've clued her in . . . It was a broken, empty-chambered weapon anyway. So far so good, the girl isn't a murderer even if she wanted to be. And there were aggravating circumstances for her fear and animosity . . . but as the guard reviewed the footage, he still felt that maybe they should do something about the girl. He didn't know what, but something. Especially at the point where one of the Baduk stones Louise Hébert was taking medicinally finally went down the wrong way and the woman began to cough and clutch at her throat (Eddy De Souza could be seen falling across the table, seizing her by the shoulders, and pounding on her back—it's probably too much to expect a North American Go Champion to be well acquainted with CPR). While Eddy was getting on with that, Xavier pulled the emergency cord and pounded on the train windows, but Laura . . . Laura De Souza was back for murder attempt number two, stuffing more stones into Madame Hébert's trembling mouth. The officer paused the tape and asked Xavier: "What's Mademoiselle De Souza shouting here?"

Xavier cleared his throat. *"He lost! He lost! How can a loser pick on another loser! Just die. Just—"*

"OK, I get the gist. This was in French?"

"Yes."

The point at which Madame Hébert lost consciousness was far from clear; the limp figure of Hébert jerked between help and harm for another minute or two as the De Souzas' tug-of-war continued. Then the transport police arrived on the scene. They did have to focus on Hébert; there was the false police tip-off, the intimidation and assault, and, of course, the sedation of her fellow passengers. But some note should probably be made about the girl as well . . .

Do Yeon-ssi muttered in Korean: "What will you write in the note? That the girl has a competitive spirit?"

Xavier was looked to for a translation, and when he didn't

provide one, the officer decided that Do Yeon-ssi was asking whether Louise Hébert was pressing charges against Laura De Souza. She wasn't. Nor the De Souzas against her.

"Laura," I said. "That was the girl's name?"

"Laura De Souza. I'll never forget."

A Laura with a jolly demeanour, hints of a horrible temper, and a strong insistence on following behavioural codes . . .

But it couldn't be. What were the odds?

Suddenly I absolutely had to see where we were, or at least get an inkling of where we were going. I stepped out of my shoes and walked across the long seat, stopping at the window and running my hands along the insides and outsides of the window casements. It really shouldn't have been that hard to access a source of light.

"Is this called Clock Carriage because the darkness is meant to reset your biorhythm?" Xavier asked. There was a smile in his voice.

"No, it's so you can take me back in time with you . . . and I was glad to go. But it's great to be back. With you and Árpád, and without a Baduk board."

Just as Xavier told me not to try to make Baduk the villain of the piece, my fingertips struck a long oval button and the blinds rustled open. He came to stand beside me. We were crossing a long iron bridge that arched across a turquoise river. The window glass was so clean and clear that it felt as if we could dive straight from the train into the water below. The sun followed us for a while, and just as it sank beneath the mossy riverbank, Árpád slunk out of the compartment. Sunset sent up ribbons of gold that looped themselves around our clasped hands and, before too long, our entwined bodies.

Sometime later the moon came up—I say "sometime" . . . it felt like only a minute, but it can't have been that quick. By then Xavier and I had ventured into the other empty compartments and found our carriage's equivalent of a restaurant car, a well-stocked pantry carriage. Fridge highlights included bottles of white wine and champagne and a bottle of vodka, and there was a dining table by the central window, also bearing gifts: a bottle of Kentucky bourbon and a tub filled to the brim with crispy pieces of salted egg fish skin. Our favourite drinking snack! Xavier lifted the tub and revealed a notecard: *To Otto and Xavier—here's to unseeing the world—Ava.*

Next we converted the carriage seats into a bed, with a zone prioritised for Árpád, who'd returned for supper and lay on his belly chewing worms, seemingly as transfixed by the graphic gleam of that night's moon as I was. The absence of light switches and accessible power sockets was intentional—all charging of devices was to be done in the pantry carriage next door. There in Clock Carriage, Xavier's phone aside, the sky was both lamp and blindfold. Cue the woo-woo perceptions: *Maybe this is what it would be like to live inside a clock, or even to be a clock,* I thought. Time would tell itself to you, bringing with it a whole host of physical memoranda, the flaring and dwindling of this orb and that. Time would crowd in close that you didn't feel it passing. "Clocks don't actually know the time," I said to Árpád. "They only repeat what they've been told."

Árpád looked round at me. A *You all right, mate?* kind of look. Xavier anthropomorphises Árpád too: at that very moment he said, "You all right, mate?" in a voice that approximated the scratchy, whistling sound of Árpád's call. Then, indicating the moon in the heavens, he added in his own voice: "I try not to look. I'd rather see it sketched or in paint. Otherwise all I can think about is the hundred and eighty something kilos of garbage we've already managed to leave up there. Ninety-six bags of piss and fecal matter . . ."

"Mucky puppies, astronauts. But you're absolutely confident, are you, that in their place you'd have managed to hold it all in until you got home?"

"Ugh . . . I know it couldn't be helped. And I don't have any better space travel waste disposal ideas. But I'm just . . . I feel bad that this is what it is to be human, Otto. To journey that far on wings so painstakingly won, all those centuries of artistic dreams and scientific thought . . . only to arrive with bags and bags of waste. In the end, that's what we produce the most of, isn't it? And maybe it's what we're best at."

He balanced his e-reader atop the "V" of his crossed ankles, reached for the vodka bottle, and poured another two shots. He's the only other person I know who can read, drink, and converse at the same time, and his drunken TED Talks take on a different character depending on what he's reading. What I really want is to get him sloshed when he's on a Wodehouse jag, to see whether he leans Jeeves-ward or Wooster-ward. But that evening it was *The Brothers Karamazov*. We were playing a drinking game within parameters he'd devised but hadn't shared with me. I just took a shot whenever he did. Whatever it was we were drinking about, he seemed to find it in every page. As if that wasn't enough, it felt like the speed of the train was accelerating the effects of the alcohol. I was leaving the pleasantly drunk phase and approaching nausea. Oh, to be like Xavier, Spera, or other friends who treat throwing up as a kind of debauchery tax that they can quickly pay before getting straight back to the merrymaking . . .

I downed the shot Xavier held out to me, swallowed hard, then took both our empty glasses and stacked them over the lid of the vodka bottle. I put the bottle out of easy reach, did the same thing with Xavier's e-reader, then rolled over, gathering him into my arms and nipping his earlobe when he grumbled that all I was going to do was nod off.

"Let's get out at the next station," Xavier said.

"Even if it's the sort of station only freight trains stop at and we have to wait days 'til we can hitch a ride back?"

"Even if by the time we get back Do Yeon-ssi's signed the house and our lives over to our friend Yuri. Let's get off this train."

"Huh. Mind telling me why?"

"At the risk of sounding like a thirty-something-looking teen-ager on *Dawson's Creek*, I just really need to know where we are."

"Well . . . you're not asking too much there."

I thought, but didn't say, that there was something vaguely

compulsive about the way that when we were together we thought and talked about anything and everything except the train we were on. But that was probably our issue, not the train's.

Instead I told him: "You're Joey, I think. Always had a soft spot for that girl."

"Say that again? Couldn't understand you, since you're already slurring . . ."

"Shhhh . . . *you're* slurring. I'm Pacey."

"You wish," he said. "You're Dawson. Don't fight it."

"Hey, I've got a train story too . . ."

"Is it from today?"

It was from the year before, when Árpád and I had attended an international mesmerism convention in Springfield, Illinois. The conference had ended, and we were on our way to New York to visit a cousin of mine who'd adopted one of Árpád's littermates. Ours was a pretty abstracted carriage. Everybody was reading or responding to written messages on phones and tablets, and Árpád was very still in the seat opposite me, wearing the special floppy-brimmed hat that slows him down while those members of the public unused to mongooses get comfortable with the idea of him. The brim of that hat is embroidered all around the inside: birds and frogs flying and hopping across a grassy vista. While Árpád was intently regarding all this, a couple boarded at Chicago's Union Station and sat across the aisle from us, both of them fresh-faced, long-haired, extensively tattooed, and engrossed in a conversation they seemed to have begun hours before. The more talkative half of the couple was an actor I recognised at once but pretended not to. The show she was on was still somewhat under the radar. Season one had been streamable for three months or so, and the buzz around it was only just building among those who'd already binged all the big shows and were searching really hard for alternatives to reruns of *Friends*. The actor's partner was a good listener, but aside from that, a mostly unknown element. The actor had hit a career speed bump, you see. She'd been the show's costar but wouldn't be returning for season two. Someone named Carla (the actor's agent, presumably) had told her it was because she was too pretty. Viewers didn't find her relatable. The actor knew there must be more to it than that; she just didn't know what. She was also strangely content with the way she looked, so undergoing any kind of procedure was out of the question. I say "strangely content" because how often do you come across someone who doesn't want to reduce this or increase that?

At any rate, the actor was saying she'd just try to get as much voice work as she could. That way, even if it took a really long time to become relatable, even if it took so long that her looks expired, at least she'd have developed as an actor. Having made this statement of intent, she laid her head on her partner's shoulder and submitted to her protective embrace. After a moment, the partner cleared her throat . . . *Uh, I think you're right, hun. It's not the way Carla says it is. Maybe I should have said something earlier, maybe not, but . . . this could all be down to that online petition.*

What petition! Show me.

The man in the seat next to mine had been eavesdropping as hard as I was, but he didn't know the actor's name or what show she appeared in. He googled *season 2 + petition*, couldn't find anything, and wordlessly acquiesced as I took the phone from him and supplied the missing terms that made the query fruitful. We studied the petition together. The number of signees correlated with the show's just-shy-of-respectable viewing figures at the time. The signees demanded that the "too pretty" actor's lines and scenarios be given to her colead, who played an ugly version of her. The tremendous attractiveness of the ugly colead was a topic for another time. Us normals are too grotesque to be seen in public, so we'd better just stay at home watching TV . . . Isn't that what such casting choices tell us? The petition saved all that for season 3 and simply argued that the silliest thing about season 1 was the division of this particular role between two actors when one of them had sufficient range to play both an ugly and a pretty version of the same person without a single costume alteration. Ostensibly, someone somewhere in the decision-making chain had listened to the viewers and had left it to the too-pretty actor's agent to let her down as gently as possible. Looking around the carriage at my fellow eavesdroppers, I could see which side each passenger was on. It was America, so people spoke up too, stopping on their way to or from the toilets or the restaurant car to express outrage at the turns mass entertainment was taking (*"What's next; will they want to decide what does and does not happen in the story? Those losers should just stick to Choose Your Own Adventure books!"*), or to tell the pretty actor they would sign a counter-petition in her favour. The actor hadn't realised how loudly she'd been talking, and she blushed all the way down to her ankles. I got her autograph to cover for my own frequent staring. It wasn't the actor I'd grown interested in, but the woman she was with. This companion's tactful and compassionate utterances indicated she was everything you could wish for in a life partner. Except that she was the very person who'd started the online petition. She must've brought it up because she couldn't quite bear going altogether incognito; it's very hard not to resist boasting about your accomplishments. I can't prove anything, I'm going on micro-expressions alone . . . but don't forget I'm hyperaware of those, having been trained to focus on them. So I stand by my observation. As we all filed off the train at Penn Station, I caught the actor's eye, gave her a bearer-of-the-gladdest-tidings-type smile and predicted that everything was going to be all right. I did the same to her partner. Both paused as they briefly contemplated battle plans, then both smiled back at me. Affirmation bright and dark. "Yes, it will, won't it?" the actor said, and her partner said: "Absolutely!"

I doubt I managed to put much of this across to Xavier. I could hear myself getting very mumbly, so maybe all Xavier picked up was "actor—petition—ankles—partner—" before I was fast asleep and he rejoined the Karamazov fraternity.

6.

The train stopped somewhere in the night. We'd left the compartment blinds up, and dozens of lamplit faces filed past our window. The station lay in darkness behind them, so it looked as if these people had burst out of the night itself with plans and schemes. Top of the list: getting everything spick-and-span, as quickly as possible. They were like a horde of sprinters carrying brooms, mops, buckets, and all manner of brushes. Laura of the sauna cubicle was standing on the station platform too, frowning as she tapped away at her tablet screen. Just as it seemed she'd be trampled, the throng broke formation, dispersing, nodding, and calling out greetings as they passed her. I waited until I was sure that they'd bypassed our carriage entirely, then drew the blinds, only momentarily considering shaking Xavier awake and reminding him he'd wanted to get out at the very next station.

Did we stop again, just before dawn? I heard the door to Clock Carriage open and close; that was what woke me up. A visit from the library car. I looked out of the window. We were still in motion, shuffling along a hilly avenue of trees. I shouldn't have been able to see that . . . I clearly recalled drawing the blinds.

Xavier opened one eye and whispered, "Are we there yet? Any lakes? How about mountains?"

I drew the blinds (again?) and nestled up against him, kissing his mouth as it curved into a smile. He went back to sleep, and I would have too if I hadn't glanced up at the luggage rack and seen the tip of Árpád's nose quivering between his suitcase and Xavier's. He'd concealed himself there so that anyone entering the compartment from the corridor wouldn't notice him until he'd sunk his claws into their head. We watched and waited, Árpád and I, my eyes on him, his eyes on the corridor, and then we heard a low-pitched, mewling growl—part fear, part fury, all mongoose. Árpád sprang to the floor and lay there in a muddle with his feet on his head. The call sounded again, this time much closer, and coming from someone who stood half a metre or so above the ground. It was Chela, huddled against the glass of the compartment door. She'd run to us. Well, to Árpád, really. I got up and let her in. I don't believe the two of them had met before, but there was no time for introductions . . . she ran in and tucked her lithe form in behind his greater bulk, a linking of forms that seemed to embolden them both. Their eyes flamed. Xavier sat up, looked over at the pair, blinked several times, and started to speak, but I'd already gone to see what Chela was running from, so I didn't hear what he said.

Someone was standing at the end of the carriageway, holding an extra-large dip net. The bag part was easily Chela- or Árpád-sized. And this someone wasn't Laura or Ava—initially I thought it might have been Allegra, the part-time passenger and part-time driver I'd been told about but hadn't seen, but . . . if anything, seeing this person was like seeing that figure waving from the barbed-wire cage as the train went by. I knew I was looking at someone, but I couldn't make out any features, no matter how I squinted. *Nonsense; they're only a few steps away, of course you can see what they look like.*

Outside the landscape stuttered. Either we'd stopped and this was what happened when my attention jerked from the window to the hallway, or we were passing a row of identical willow trees one by one. The person holding the net began walking towards me. I wanted to run back into the compartment and build a barricade. But rationality continued to speak to me. It said: *Otto, that string bag is Chela- or Árpád-sized, but you're not. You're significantly bigger and heavier than this person. And don't you see, they're gripping the handle of their net with both hands—since when was a dip net a deadly weapon? Besides, this person is wearing fuzzy slippers and peacock green pajamas, and if those intimidate you, I don't know what else to tell you. If you've got even a millimetre of backbone in you, you'll walk forward right this minute.*

I went forward, all right, but those rational points only enlarged the sight problem. It wasn't at all like looking at a person through a hazy filter. There wasn't any kind of incongruity shock either: they were just there, quite at one with their surroundings, even smiling. In recognition, it seemed. I smiled too, though I didn't think I knew anybody who'd run around in the middle of the night frightening mongooses by way of amusement.

It was as if this person was both *behind* my eyes and in front of them. I kept catching myself in the act of assembling the image at the very moment it appeared . . . That makes it all sound more voluntary than it felt. Someone was moving towards me. Someone visible; I couldn't simply choose not to see them. Yet to see them I had to do more than just look. A lot more. Whatever it was I had to do, the attempt put every cell of my sight apparatus under such strain that I felt blood vessels bursting. I wobbled forward, putting out a hand a couple of times to touch the wall panels, which vibrated as my fingers crossed them. The train was still moving, then. The person stopped smiling once I got close enough to pull the dip net out of his hands and tell him we were trying to get some sleep.

"So was I," he said. "Well, goodnight for now."

Moving too quickly for me to stop him, he whipped the carriage door open. Not the one that would've led back into the carriage car, but the one that would've opened out onto a platform if we'd been stationary. We both staggered as the wind whirled in at around a hundred kilometres per hour to besport itself right merrily, roaring with laughter as it did all it could to rip the hair from our scalps and the skin from our faces—and then he jumped out of the train. He sprang out into thin air; I spun around to find and pull the nearest emergency cord so I didn't see him fall. And mine was the second cord pull—behind me, Xavier had found one first.

"He jumped," I said, but the train was screaming. I don't think Xavier heard me over the bumping of the door hinge and the muddy baritone of the railway brake. "Did you see— He said he couldn't sleep or something—and then he fucking jumped . . ."

We ground to a halt, and a chorus of shouts grew in volume, along with the rumble of heavy footfall as tens of people scrambled down from the train and ran along the side of it in unison. The maintenance team was still with us.

It was very early on Sunday morning, and I was standing in the middle of the carriageway wearing nothing but a pair of boxers with the Czech word for Saturday on them, shivering spasmodically and staring with bloodshot eyes as I waved an extra-large dip net and shouted about somebody jumping off the train while it was still moving. Laura's voice came over the tannoy telling us to stay exactly where we were. Xavier did what any kind soul would have done and made me get dressed before the train operator inquisition began. We tried to get our story straight. "Tell me again," he said. I told him again. Then a third time, and a fourth time. He was shaking too. But he kept asking, "But who, Otto? Who was chasing Chela with a net? Who opened the carriage door?"

He held my head between his hands and looked into my eyes; I watched him reviewing what he knew. I'd been standing over him when I woke up, with Chela already in our compartment. And he'd got out into the hallway in time to see me running at the carriage door, but that was all.

It could have been me, just messing about on my own. I could've frightened Chela in an effort to do Árpád a favour by driving a mating prospect right into his arms. As for wrenching the door open and attempting a flying leap—another neural blip, just like running into a burning house for no bloody reason.

"Wondering how long you can put up with somebody who

keeps going in for completely unnecessary heroics?" I asked, jocularly but really not joking at all. When Xavier gets tired of me all he has to do is take his pick from the queue of suitors I pretend not to feel threatened by.

"I've actually got a lot of time for people like that," he said. "And anyway, I'm . . . well, you're the one who could do a lot better."

I kissed him. "What are you talking about? Listen, I'm gonna go a bit Anne Brontë on you. Are you ready?"

"Will you let me off if I say I'm not ready?"

"No. A Brontean moment can never be averted. I prefer your faults to other people's perfections, Xavier Shin. There. That wasn't so bad, was it?"

He was meant to laugh, make a face, parse the sentence, kiss me back, any combination of those four. But he looked at the floor, thinking.

"Xavier?"

We were interrupted by a princess in her late twenties. I'll amend that slightly: an haute urban princess with a side ponytail, her blue tulle ballgown slashed at the hip and pulled on over silk leggings. A tiny emerald shone from the piercing in her left nostril, but her feet crowned the entire look: she wore an astonishingly white pair of Converse. Trainers only ever stay as clean as the conscience of their wearer.

She climbed up into our carriage from the track and stood in front of us with folded arms.

"Allegra Yu," she said. "What happened, exactly?" She—or perhaps Ava—had drawn a heart-shaped beauty spot onto the highest point of each of her cheekbones, amplifying the seamless asymmetries of her face so that she wore several expressions at once. She had a Peckham accent, which made me think she might actually hear me out. Peckhamites are deep. You'll get hurt if you try to waste their time, but otherwise they are available for soul-to-soul communication, giving compassionate audience to all manner of monologues delivered in languages they don't speak. What am I basing these claims on? I'll just flash my son-of-a-Peckhamite credentials here.

Allegra listened to what I had to say without asking anything, though at a couple of points she did make some intensely questioning eye contact with me and also with Xavier. After I'd fallen silent, she took the dip net from me. I must have been waving it again as I spoke. I was quite willing to relinquish the net but found that my fingers had other ideas; Allegra had to peel them away from the handle. I was not behaving like a reliable witness.

"Anything to add?" she asked Xavier.

He looked her in the eyes. "No. That's what happened."

"You saw it all?"

"Yeah."

"OK," she said. "Well, we're looking. I'll let you know if we find . . . anything."

"If?" I said. "What do you mean, 'if'?"

"Good question," she said, and considerably disconcerted me by putting a hand into the pocket of her ballgown, pulling out a lollipop, jamming it into the left corner of her mouth, and continuing without answering my "good question": "Stay inside the train, please. I'll need to see you both a bit later."

"Can't wait," I said. "But for now . . . can I have a lollipop too?"

She switched her lollipop from the left to the right side, said it was her last one, and rejoined the crew milling around the exterior. She took the dip net with her.

Árpád and Chela believed me. The one skipped up onto my knee and waited until I lowered my head for grooming, brushing my fringe back and forth as he checked for nits. The other came and put her paw in my hand for a second.

"Xavier," I said, "this is Chela, our future daughter-in-law."

In Korean, Xavier asked Chela to take care of him in times to come. She listened impassively, and when he went to pat her on the head, she ducked—because of the pressure I'd just put on her with my introduction, Xavier said. Then the two mongooses bounded out of the carriage door and along the track.

7.

I don't know how this makes us sound—I don't know how any
of it makes us sound—but the next thing on our agenda was
breakfast. An unknown man had jumped out of the train right
in front of my eyes, but when Xavier asked if I was hungry, I
said I could do with some French toast.

Xavier was chef for the morning; we'd flipped a coin. We
walked into the pantry car, and eggshells crunched beneath our
feet. The yolks and whites ran down the window in viscous
stripes. A loaf of brioche sat in a pot on the hob, submerged in
milk and sprinkled with violet leaves. The butter dish was in the
sink. The stub of butter left in there had been thoroughly licked;
tongue marks aside, you could tell from its foamy veneer of spit.
There was maple syrup all over the place; it had been rubbed and
drizzled over every drawer and cupboard handle, mixed with
butter for additional slip. This was bespoke vandalism, a project
completed by somebody who'd known we'd want French toast
in the morning and gone out of their way to incorporate every

ingredient we'd need. Mind you, all the ingredients had been gifts from our host in the first place. A case of Ava giveth and Ava taketh away?

I started cleaning up, but Xavier stopped me. "Even if they don't find any trace of your jumping man, Allegra should at least see this."

"Well, anyone inclined to believe that there was no jumping man would think I did this too."

"Well, they'd be wrong. I don't know about anything else, but you'd never waste food."

"True."

Our hands were sticky, so we washed them in the shower car. But then he found syrup on my collarbone, and I found some in his navel, and we just kept finding more and more, so getting truly clean took ages. Particularly when you factor in the way shower acoustics can augment your lover's breathing, adding a stroke to every one of your strokes, sending the sound of him tingling along your skin as you feel him come. Getting fully dressed again was a struggle too. Eventually he picked up his clothes and walked out of the shower car, laughing and telling me he'd dress outside the door.

I pulled my jeans on, then patted the pocket. Xavier's phone was in there. He'd taken my pre-shower clothing and left me his. There was still no cellular signal, but quickly, before he realised his mistake, I keyed in his passcode, opened up his message inbox, and read the top two messages—the ones that had come in while we'd been talking to Do Yeon-ssi when we first boarded the train. Those were the only two I had eyes for. The first one, which had come in just before he'd asked how Yuri and Do Yeon-ssi had met, said: *Tip: you do know me.* The second one, which had arrived just in time to change Xavier's "We don't know Yuri" to "We don't know what we'd do without Yuri" said: *Really? After all I've done for you?*

An imposter with an assumed name was in our home right at this very moment, cosying up to Do Yeon-ssi. And based on these two text messages, sent from a number that wasn't even saved as a contact in his phone, Xavier had advocated a wait-and-see attitude towards the situation. He'd even mentioned the possibility that this "Yuri" meant well. I didn't get it. While it's possible to receive an unsigned message from an unknown number that's so distinctive you immediately recognise the sender, these two were hardly that. Anybody could have sent them, but Xavier had identified the sender in that split-second middle-of-the-night-phone-call way. You know—your phone rings in the middle of the night. The screen tells you the number is withheld or unknown, and you don't usually answer such calls, but it's so late that the caller could have some spectacular news that will change everything—for better, or for worse. You answer the phone. You say, "Hello? Hello?" but nobody speaks. And then you say a name and add a question mark. It's not about who you really think is calling, or even who you hope is calling. It's got nothing to do with logical inferences that can be drawn from the events of the past few hours. It's about what simply is. You say the name that's been on your mind from waking to sleeping. The fact that I obviously wasn't that person for Xavier didn't bother me too much—he wasn't that person for me either. The association is rarely positive. What's notable is that it's intense. I couldn't ask about it; Xavier had to tell me of his own accord.

It came down to this: I dare not risk a jealous scene. Where would the underwhelming product of a loving home find the nerve to be anything other than meek in this scenario? Everything was in place both nature- and nurture-wise for me to show aptitude at something, somehow, somewhere. I don't lose much sleep over not having done that (yet?), but the romantic attachment failures are a sore spot. That's a field in which I really ought not underwhelm. When Martha and Lieselotte had me, Martha's legal name was still Mark, and Lieselotte was a high court judge in Bern. They're two of the freest people I know, and somehow that seems like a by-product of the rambling conversation they've been in ever since they met, an exchange that draws them down by-lanes of trivia and scholarship, pettiness and poetry. When some new pact clicks into place, they meet at its corner to kiss. My professor mum made her Martha-ness official, and my Bern high court judge mum stepped down and stripped her view of justice all the way down to grass roots, serving her god (and I really do think justice is a god for Lieselotte) as a police inspector who does her paperwork whilst sipping coffee out of a mug emblazoned with a picture of her wife and son. I hate that mug. The picture on it makes us look like Ikea models who might just get thrown in as freebies if you buy enough furniture. But catalog elements aside, it's a photo in which Martha is full-on sultry professor, and I look like a cute baby Viking. So even if her current mug gets broken, or hidden, Lieselotte just pulls out another, identical one.

I wanted to be like that, and as I say, I should've been able to.

But lasting six months with anyone was a miracle. Or so I'd thought, until Xavier. We'd worked out our key factor: absolute trust. That's what Lieselotte and Martha have. I don't think they'd have secretly looked at each other's messages, though. Round and round I went, bursting the last few soap bubbles clustered along the outside of the shower stall as I tried to come up with a way to ask about this. To ask so Xavier would hear that I wanted to help him deal with whatever effect this "Yuri" was having on him. If he even wanted or needed help with that. Ugh. I looked in the mirror; my eyes were getting more bloodshot by the second. I closed them and pressed my knuckles down over my eyelids, trying to visualise that face one more time. The face of the man with the dip net. I saw something like a flame; a sizzling wave that melted matter. My lungs creaked, turning to cork again. My mouth filled with smoke; I coughed, still trying to look. He was there, I could find him, I just had to hold my breath a little longer, just—

My chin hit the basin and then the floor. I curled up, coughing and coughing. Xavier knocked on the door.

"Otto? You all right?"

I knew I had to open my eyes if I wanted to breathe. And I did want to breathe. Didn't I? Xavier knocked again. Breathe, breathe. My eyes opened. "Yeah, I'll be out in a sec. I've got your phone."

When I stood up again my eyes looked even worse; redder than red. There was hardly any white left around the pupil. Xavier had left his sunglasses on the ledge above the sink, so I put those on too.

Out in the corridor, I gave his phone back to him, he checked the screen, then said he wanted me to see the postal-sorting car. He had the tub of salted egg fish skin from the pantry tucked in under his other arm. We ate as we went along, slowing so that Xavier could stop in a doorway with his arm stuck out, seeking a signal: "Just wondering if our friend Yuri happens to know what's going on . . ."

Bringing Yuri up first . . . that was something.

"You do know who this Yuri is, yeah? It may not seem like it, but I do worry about Do Yeon-ssi."

"Oh, please . . . you should be more worried about what'll happen to Yuri if my aunt finds out he's with her under false pretences. But I do have some idea who he is, yeah."

"Any idea why he's put himself on a fast track to adoptive nephewhood?"

He looked at me quickly, then looked away. "It's his pattern, I guess. It's like he tries to get the best out of you, and if it doesn't work, he just . . . goes."

"He's an ex?"

"Why do you ask that whenever I mention a friend you haven't heard about? You do realise that hardly any of my friends are exes?"

"I do. But back to Yuri . . . is *he* an ex?"

"If he is who I think he is, then yeah," Xavier muttered. Each syllable begrudged.

"The most recent one?"

"Yeah."

"Maybe he wants to get back together," I said, as calmly as I could.

He said something under his breath, then, much more audibly: "You don't seem to have an ex like that, Otto. An ex who makes you feel like shit."

"No, I don't have an ex like that. But there are always the ones who try, so I think I know what you're talking about."

Xavier grimaced. "It wasn't . . . He didn't—I'm talking about a dynamic where someone's only ever quietly, steadily good to you, you keep fucking up, and they accept it. Never cross or negative . . ."

I must have looked skeptical, because he repeated: "Never. He never showed it, but there's no way I didn't hurt him with my shitty behaviour. And don't say I probably didn't fuck up as much as I think I did. You weren't there."

"I wasn't. But I'm here now, and the shitty-boyfriend routine doesn't sound like you. If that was really your style, it would've come out by now. Can you give me an example?"

"Maybe some other time," he said. He stared out of the window and started eating his feelings; a stack of crispy fish skins disappeared in one bite. Then he coughed and flung an arm out, almost dropping his phone: "Lake! A lake—"

We'd ground to a halt in what looked like a junkyard or a fairground—possibly one in the process of conversion into the other, but both projects had been halted, so the track was surrounded by what seemed like miles of rusting machinery, dust-matted pieces of apparatus and hulking shapes swaddled in oilcloth. But immediately beyond that first layer, just like looking through the pillars of a grey-brown gate, the bright, crisp colours of the lake basin curved around to meet the eye. It was quite a violent blue, that lake. A colour that ripped the horizon. Some lakes are calm, and some are tense. This one was a thunderous mass at war with the sky, David shaking a watery fist at Goliath and roaring, *I'll drown you!*

We jumped down from the carriage and walked lakeward but were only a few yards from the train when Allegra walked into view, wearing a hard hat and muttering into a walkie-talkie that muttered back at her. She raised a hand when she saw us, made gestures instructing us to reboard the train, then turned and paced the other way without even checking to see if she was being obeyed. She didn't need to. We weighed up the numbers . . . maintenance team under Allegra's command versus us. We went back.

"Are we . . . prisoners?" I asked Xavier.

"Probably not," he said, trying to take a picture of the lake from the carriage doorway. He couldn't get the angle right and gave up. "Though if we are, I'm sure Allegra will let us know."

A series of message alerts flashed across his phone screen. "Signal!"

He called Do Yeon-ssi without even looking at the messages. She answered on the second ring, and he put her on speakerphone. "I was just thinking about my nephews . . . where are you? How's Árpád? Did you get hold of Ava? Are you having a nice time?"

She broke off between questions to sing along, with word-perfect recall, to the "Macarena."

"Everything's great," Xavier said. "What about Yuri? He's behaving himself, right?"

"We're getting on. He's really . . . unmaterialistic, you know? I thought he'd come to fill his pockets with everybody else's money . . . Nothing wrong with that, as long as you play fair, of course. But he's playing for charity donations."

"Oh? Which charities?" I asked.

(Xavier scowled at me and whispered "What do you care which charities . . . ?")

"Ask him yourself," Do Yeon-ssi said. "You didn't call him?"

"We haven't had signal!"

"Do you know, last night Yuri made a bet with me that you wouldn't call him. He said something about feeling a bit left out ever since you two had become a couple."

Xavier said nothing, I said nothing. I needed to think about it a bit more, the claim Saint Yuri had on the person I loved. Some mutation of guilt that I couldn't get my non-Catholic head around at all.

Do Yeon-ssi got brusque with us. "This is the first time I've ever had to tell you to treat your friends properly. Call him now, OK?"

"Will do. Wish we were there doing the 'Macarena' with you," I told her.

"No you don't. And anyway, I've got Yuri."

We hung up.

"Silly me for wanting to go back early," Xavier said. "She's got Yuri now, and things have never been better."

He remembered his text and e-mail alerts and thumbed through them.

"Any from Yuri?"

"Nah."

"You're not gonna call?"

"You're as bad as Do Yeon-ssi." He knocked on the door of the next carriage and waited a couple of seconds before leading me into a carriage that was wall-to-wall wooden trays, each tray stuffed to overflow with letters and labelled with the names of villages and boroughs within cities. The desk in here was a long, narrow writing desk, not a dance floor. There were plenty of drawers and built-in stationery receptacles, and a little row of language dictionaries. Latin, Italian, modern Greek, and so on. Three chairs were drawn up around it, and each letter writer had carved their name around the edge of the table closest to their chair. Allegra. Laura. Ava. Ava had mentioned she was having a peculiar few years. Years lived out on this train with two people who wouldn't let her talk to anybody but wrote letters alongside her? That sign must have said HELP and not HELLO after all; I'd been an idiot to take her word for it.

Beneath the first window of the carriage, the wall wedged inward and held two baskets with an engraved slot above each one. The OUT basket held a handful of envelopes, and the IN basket contained one envelope, addressed to the train itself, *The Lucky Day*.

"All these letters . . ." I looked over at the wooden trays. "They're to the train?"

Xavier opened one of the drawers, labelled "Chaouen," and took out an envelope. *Dear Lucky Day*, he read aloud, converting French into English as he read,

Everything is fucked, I don't even know where to start with how
fucked everything is. I saw you waiting here at the station, the

*Lucky Day, my lucky day, and I almost came in at your door so
you could take me away. But I have to stay and see this through.
That's what's best for everyone. Even though it isn't me you've
come for today, train, you can carry this along with you.*

Thanks.

*PS—Don't write back. I've heard you do that sometimes,
but you can't try that with me. I know trains can't write. Nor
read, for that matter.*

I opened a drawer labelled "Croydon" and read,

*To Whom It May Concern, I am flabbergasted to see you
flaunting the fruit of ill-gotten gains. Those of your generation
may see the Lucky Day as a "cool hangout," but I will forever
be reminded of the Sichuan Affair that made paupers of tens of
families and disgraced hundreds more, all so Hardeep and Shilpa
Kapoor could walk away with their scavenged millions. Hope
you crash and burn, and I don't mean that metaphorically.*

R. Pandey.

". . . Does Ava basically have to stay onboard so she can't be
tracked to a fixed address?"

"I wonder," Xavier said. "Quite a few of the letters reference
this Sichuan Affair. There's a subset that feels robbed every time
they see this train. And their versions of the Affair are quite different. When you said we aren't allowed to talk to Ava, I wondered if it was to protect her from employees of these lovely pen

pals of hers. But if you think about it, the letters are just hot air. To post them you have to walk straight up to the train and push them through the slot. You could just as easily say all this to her face or give her a slap or whatever else is on your mind. That could backfire, though, and they just want a risk-free way of making her feel bad, so they sneak up to the train and post letters like this, presumably when there's no one else around. So yeah, there are those letters, but most of the ones I saw made me laugh or go 'awww' or 'OK, that's very niche' . . . "

I knew what he meant, having rifled through a few more drawers at random while he told me about them. "This one, for example, commending her choice of transport and trashing air, road, and sea transport. *The sea is particularly lethal; perhaps it's angry with mankind for wriggling out of the water all those aeons ago and choosing land. Now it's all sharks and naval mines in there . . . "*

"Still thinking about the Sichuan Affair," Xavier said, picking up the envelopes in the OUT box and fanning them out across the desktop "What was the name of that 'fruit of ill-gotten gains' letter writer again?"

I went back to the Croydon tray: "R. Pandey."

He flicked the corner of one envelope and dropped the other four back into the OUT box and reached for a letter opener.

"Want to see Ms. Kapoor's reply?"

The sunglasses had slipped down the bridge of my nose; I pushed them back up. "It somehow feels like we're in trouble anyway, so why not . . ."

Ava got stressed out when people maligned her train. She'd

pressed down so hard with her pen that the paper had torn in places.

Hi R. Pandy!

Well, this is nice, my fortieth letter from you. I think it's forty, but I've lost count, which you can't blame me for, given that you use aliases. Sorry it's taken so long to write back. Were those paint bombs little love letters from you too? Here I am, you've smoked me out at last.

Yes, Hardeep and Shilpa Kapoor were monstrosities, weren't they! Number one morality tale for me and my cousins growing up. They're every error we could possibly make conveniently packaged up in two bodies. Do you know how they died? One stumbled into the path of a horse-drawn carriage, and the other—you'll like this, R. Pande—the other choked on emeralds. They left two sons behind. The eldest was fathered by Hardeep, and the younger son was a Caucasian-Indian mix. You can think Hardeep's stumble was deliberate if you want, but I think he was so plastered he had no idea he was out in the middle of a main road. For months he'd been drinking the costliest imported liquor round the clock. A perpetual celebration; he'd had the privilege of being well and truly blackmailed. Not that the blackmailer would have seen what he did as anything special. It was a routine sequence, sweeping a smuggler's wife off her feet, threatening said smuggler with public circulation of wifey's love letters, and, even more pathetically, sealing the deal by promising to disappear from her life if furnished with all the vital names, dates, and places crucial to the smuggling routes. You don't have to put in much effort to blackmail weaklings who don't feel like they can live without their even weaker wives. You can lead the weakling around the teahouses he frequents and use him like a pair of spectacles you look through to see the hidden design laid out on every low table, the meaning of the distance or proximity between the celadon teacup and the white one. The variations usually took years to learn, but blackmail gave Hardeep formidable teaching ability; his blackmailer boasted that it only took him about a month to absorb all the teacup arrangement codes necessary for tracking sea shipments without moving from his spot in the shade under the bamboo trees.

If you ask me, R. Pandi, his associates were stupid to have let him host a quarter of the bankroll. He was a notably fragile link in that smuggling chain from the beginning. We haven't found that he had a reputation for financial greed . . . it seems he had that much going for him. But he was too impulsive and had no discipline at all. That's what the people who knew him well said about him. Lucky for him, then, that the only activity he liked more than drinking was successfully falsifying document after document, undaunted by intricacy or time frame. The Sichuan tea handlers couldn't find anything to dislike about Hardeep and Shilpa as a couple—that was another factor in their favour. They get mentioned in a few letters as a local golden couple, and that must have been the first impression they gave as an attractive, well-mannered pair come over from Assam to talk tea in fluent Mandarin. That was the only reason he rose up the ranks the way he did, and after the East India Company crushed the cooperation among their competitors, Hardeep had nothing to do but buy liquor. Yes, as you said, he got to keep the money. He got to flee to Newcastle and live in lavish anonymity. And the wife he'd done it all for stayed where the money was. Run after the East India Company agent? Not Shilpa Kapoor. Let the letters she'd written to him be read aloud to her night after night; she could listen to it all stone-cold sober. This would usually happen at around one in the morning, with Hardeep putting on a simpering voice to impersonate her. "Ha ha," she said, and "I don't care," and "Well, I'm going to be happy anyway." She applauded her own turns of phrase. It was too late to do anything else. For about a decade Shilpa and Hardeep were serious about putting the money to good use. We have a lot of the documentation for funds and scholarships; they looked at and approved plans for schools and orphanages. It looks like the scammers of every age find a way to make our money do the most damage where we want and need it to do the most good—so in the age of private philanthropy, falling prey to scammers meant sponsoring altruistic fronts for some hair-raising shit.

The atonement funding paper trail dwindled to nothing after about a decade, as if Hardeep and Shilpa ultimately conceded that they simply didn't have an eye for an honest endeavour. And why would they, if that "birds of a feather flock together" saying holds true? Shilpa already had some emeralds, but those were love gifts, so she bought herself some more; they were best suited to her colouring. She didn't wear them; they were last-ditch emeralds. The sort her type of woman would put on before being led to the guillotine and displayed before a baying crowd. Shilpa dwelt on her new emeralds and dwelt in them. She inspected their inclusions through a jeweller's eyeglass. She was worried that they'd been switched for fakes when she wasn't looking. When she wasn't worrying about that she worried that someone would come and take her emeralds from her outright. Someone might even kill her for them. And she didn't necessarily think they'd be wrong to, so she wouldn't even be able to come back as a protesting ghost. So Shilpa took to hiding her emeralds in her mouth. This was noticed, especially when she spoke. Hardeep was so drunk all the time he just thought her teeth had turned green and went on forcing her to relive the litany of passionate declarations she'd never made to him. Of course, once you start hiding emeralds in your mouth, you're done for. It's no great leap from there to sleeping with your emeralds in your mouth, which is how Shilpa Kapoor choked one night. She'd hidden away for the night in a wardrobe full of fur coats. Nobody heard her choking, or so they say, and she wasn't found until morning. None of this made too much of a dent in those scavenged millions you mentioned. Not the emeralds, not the liquor, not the attempts at philanthropy, not anything else they bought.

But that doesn't actually matter, R. Pandee, because we don't know where those two hid the rest of those millions. If you want full updates on the search, though, I'm sure my mother or one of my aunts or uncles could fill you in. You've written to someone whose family hasn't moved house for centuries in case the treasure is somewhere in the house. We're not a small family, so we branched out down the street and then down the neighbouring street, and so on. Charles Dickens heard about us and tried to find out more whilst in the region, but he backed down after a bunch of brown-skinned and muscle-bound Tyneside lads visited him at his hotel and advised him to write a sequel to *Oliver Twist* instead.

My mum's chronicles would probably be quite different. She wants to give the pilfered fortune back to those it was taken from; it's just that she has to find it first. So off she goes around the world, chasing clues and visiting charlatans who promise to help her reclaim our family honour. We haven't spoken for years. This Sichuan Affair of ours is a truly deep-rooted daftness.

Respectfully speaking, R. Pan D (just as respectfully as you wished we'd crash and burn), I've told you all this because seeing a train and getting yourself hyped up about some 1737 events you don't really understand is not too far off from using your mouth as a gemstone safe.

<u>Sufficient unto the day is the evil thereof</u>, and so on,

Ava Kapoor

"Which part of this is most likely to make R. Pandey grind their teeth to dust?" Xavier asked, waving his hand over the pages like a gleeful conjurer.

I rubbed my chin. "Well, Xavier, I'd say it'll be the relentless misspelling of the surname. You?"

"I reckon it'll be the overall tone . . . you know . . . the explain-ingness of it all. *Let's just live quiet lives, OK, shithead?*" He kissed his fingers at the sheets of paper before slipping them back into the envelope. Then we rolled up our sleeves, more than half-convinced that the scavenged millions were hidden somewhere on the train. Maybe even in this very carriage . . .

We were just uncertain what currency it would be in. Maybe it was millions of won worth of emeralds?

"Never mind the format," Xavier said. "There'll be a lot of it, and that's how we'll know we've found it."

We called out to Árpád and Chela, hoping elite search abilities were a characteristic that mongooses shared. Árpád Montague XXX doesn't give up until he finds what he's looking for. His approach is very in-depth, though, so you have to be resigned to the things around you never looking the same again after the search. It was probably just as well that a couple of seconds after Xavier called in the mongooses (and they failed to appear) Allegra Yu's voice came through the tannoy speaker above our heads, pro-posing we meet her in the picture gallery car in five minutes.

8.

The picture gallery was just next door, and windowless. A low-hanging lightbulb simulated wintry sunshine; each of the canvases were bathed in white. There was one on each wall, and they were paired. The two blank, unframed canvases faced each other, and so did two scratchily pigmented paintings, both portraits. It looked as if the painter had tried to scrape away every other line he laid down. But this discordance was gentle; the colours pledged to settle at the touch of a hand. Xavier approached the head-and-shoulders portrait first; quite confrontationally, I thought. I could see what was making him nervous. The subject of the portrait looked as if he was somewhere in his early twenties, his clean-shaven cheeks heavy with puppy fat. He appeared to be leaning back and to the side, deliberately avoiding either the centre of the frame or the light in front of it. He also appeared to be looking at Xavier. There was merriment and malice in those unblinking sloe-black eyes. I tucked my hand into the back pocket of Xavier's jeans, and we stood almost nose to nose with the portrait, trying to stare it down together. The man in the painting was dark haired, ruddy of skin, and bushy of eyebrow. Whichever way I tilted my head, Xavier was the only one of us I could catch him looking at. A lock of hair fell over his left eye, just like a lock of mine fell over my right eye. I'd sometimes tuck or blow the lock out of the way, but this guy would probably just have stared at you through it. The white shirt he wore was mostly unbuttoned, revealing that he either waxed his chest or hadn't bothered to paint the hair in. *I bet that was a constant—starting things you couldn't finish*, I thought. Then wondered about my confident use of the past tense, and my verdict that this was a self-portrait. One more thing: I'd seen him somewhere. One, two, three, the facts I knew.

"Was he giving you the eye like this when you were here yesterday?"

Xavier nodded. "The expression was a bit different, though. Probably just my mood."

"Different how?"

Xavier didn't answer.

I turned to face the portrait that was hanging on the opposite wall. It was of a father and son. Their resemblance was unmistakable, and the setting was presumably the father's study; there were lots of books and box files, and a theremin dimly visible behind the desk. The father was seated with an arm thrown proudly around his son, who was standing and looking at him with a mixture of affection and reserve. The son was the subject of the self-portrait behind me, and in this portrait with his father he was younger still. About ten. They'd been much older when I saw them in the flesh, but I had seen them both. Five years ago.

Not together like this, smiling at each other—

Their faces loomed before me, stretched, contracted. In a whirl of black hair and blue tulle, Allegra was there, both hands beneath my elbow, propping me up and twisting me away from the canvas. If she hadn't, I'd have staggered into it head-first.

Xavier's back was to me, and he looked round. "Who are they?" he asked. His face showed . . . I'm not sure. Not worry, exactly. Sadness. Seriousness.

"That's Přemysl Stojaspal," Allegra said, pointing at the self-portrait and at the ten-year-old portrayed standing beside his father. "And that's his father, Karel. Both painted by Přem. You seem to recognize them, Otto?"

"I'll tell you, but tell me something first—"

"No, Otto." Allegra was shaking her head. "I'm afraid not, mate. You don't get on a train, put us behind schedule with a search for a jumper there's no trace of, then get to set the pace of the questioning."

"So you didn't find anything. That was what I wanted to know."

Just as it had been with the man in the fire. The one I'd rushed in to rescue. At least that was how it had seemed at the time: it felt like I had to get him out of there, I had to because nobody else could. I'd seen him in the window—a motionless figure. Přemysl. He had seen me, had given me a look of terror. I thought, *Why doesn't he run?* Maybe fright had glued him to the ground, inflating his eyes and the "o" of his mouth, hollowing his muscles and pouring itself through them. He stared down, I stared up, a cupboard fell (on him? behind him?), and I ran in through the main door of the house—which was where I'd seen Karel, his father, on the stairs. The wheezing, grey-faced man, thrusting his cane further up along the banisters to try to speed his progress, the flies around him—I will always remember them as having flown out of his open jaws, even though I know that can't have happened. The old man's breath in my face as he pulled at my jacket and said: "My son. Please . . ." I'm not sure what he said next. I talked about this with the psychiatrist I got referred to afterwards; it's fairly similar to Xavier wavering between readings of Ava's sign. I think the man said, *Please help my son*, but I also heard *Please stop my son*. The psychiatrist said I might have conflated meanings into one word. Meanings that disorganised my hearing. I'd stopped the discussion there, because both of the meanings were moot; the flat was empty, and running in there didn't help or stop anyone.

"Otto? It seems as if you've seen Karel and Přem before?"

"You already said that," I muttered.

"I'm giving you another chance to answer while it's just us. Laura's on her way over, and there are things it's better not to discuss in front of her. So if you know anything, Otto, it's important to say so now. Please."

Watching her as she spoke, I saw what I'd missed in our first encounter, when she'd mostly been listening. A current flickered across that billion-facet face; the kind generated by habitual flow between two opposing thoughts (or future events?). One troubled her, and the other got her all overjoyed. She couldn't choose which would prevail, so she made preparations that removed her from the present and placed her one step ahead of us. But only one. She exhibited the top two characteristics I look for in those who book

hypnotism sessions with me: marked inattention towards imme-
diate surroundings and heightened sensory arousal. It's even better (from a lazy hypnotist's perspective) when one is linked to or
caused by the other. In short, Allegra Yu was highly suggestible.

"They're friends of Ava's, aren't they?" I said. "The composer
and . . ."

"They were friends of mine too. Přem's a dabbler, but mostly
he ran the publishing house his father set up. Until he disappeared."

"When was that?" Xavier asked.

"Well, the last time anybody we know of spoke to him in person was about five years ago. The summer of 2014. There've been
e-mails and phone conversations since, mostly to do with the publishing house, but the house has had to drop him because they're
almost sure the person e-mailing and taking calls isn't actually
him, and they can't really work with a mystery publisher, no matter how efficient. When did you see him, Otto?"

(The summer of 2014. The fire was in July.)

"Who? Přem? I've never seen him," I said.

The firefighters had found no one in the flat, and the man
who'd called them, the same man who'd asked me to help or
stop his son, told them he was there to collect post; he said he'd
known his son wasn't at home. He couldn't remember exactly
what he'd said to me, but he thought it must have been something
like *That's my son's flat.* I couldn't let myself believe that that old
man was lying, but it felt even less possible that he was telling the
truth. And actually I didn't need to know what kind of event I had
experienced that day, as long as it was never revived or repeated.

"If only you knew how much you sound like Ava right now."
Allegra reached up, took off my sunglasses, and continued un-
fazed by my devil-red eyes: "That's why Karel gave her these
paintings; she kept asking what Přem looked like. She wouldn't
speak to Přem, and she'd look at a chair he was sitting in or an
area he was standing in, then say there wasn't anyone there. It got
a bit creepy. I think Přem was freaked out by it as well, so the atmosphere was a bit prickly until she finally let the joke go."

Ava had told me about playing her theremin to a vacant room.
Now it sounded like she'd never stopped considering the room
vacant; she'd only stopped mentioning that aspect to those who
were uncomfortable with it.

Allegra paused when Xavier asked about photos of Přem. "If
you give each other significant looks after I say this I'm kicking
you both off the train right now, but . . . when Přem went missing,
we tried to dig up photos of him, and there aren't any."

"Not a single photo, eh," I said.

"Of someone who walked this earth for over thirty years,"
Xavier said.

It was only the viewpoint that had changed; I'd moved my
whole body, not just my head. Xavier had switched positions too.
That was why the self-portrait now appeared to be looking at
Allegra. Those were the reasons, the very good reasons, for the
apparent alteration; Přemysl was not going to look at me next, no,
no, nothing of the sort.

I copied his focus on Allegra, who was telling us: "Look, now
that we don't spend time together anymore I feel like there's some-

thing fishy about the lack of photos as well. And other things come to mind, all sorts of niggling things I suddenly want to bother him about and have him explain away. For example, look at those paintings . . . Přem made them too. He got rid of all the others, so these are the only ones left."

She gestured towards the two blank canvases, a narrow streak of white above each of the connecting doors.

"They're not paintings," Xavier said, after a moment. "Unless? We're looking at white paint on white canvas or some similar abstraction?"

"Abstraction?" Allegra said tiredly. "No. Just tell me what's in the paintings."

I looked up and to the left, swivelled, then looked up and to the right. I saw white unbroken by even the faintest hint of an outline. Perhaps there was something notable about the smoothness and density of texture, but that wasn't something you could say was "in" the paintings.

"Why don't you just tell us?"

"No, you have to say it. Look at the one to the left and talk. Just say whatever comes into your head."

I surrendered first: "OK, but all I can see is an axe about the length of my arm with a ribbon tied into a bow around the handle. What . . . ?"

Allegra grabbed a fistful of her own hair and nodded.

Xavier stared up at the canvas too, closed his eyes tightly, opened them again and said: "Sorry, but I can't see that the axe is sketched in grayscale, but the ribbon's ruby red—"

"Wah," I said. Because even after hearing his description and my own, all I saw was a white canvas . . . and, it seemed, an image that had utterly bypassed my eyes and flowed straight into words.

"And to the right?" Allegra said. "You can't pause. Keep looking and keep saying what you're thinking."

"But, Allegra, what devilry is this?" Xavier said, eyes probing the canvas from corner to corner. "Does everybody you ask to look into this white box tell you it's an utter blank in the centre of which is a gamine brown woman with an ecstatic smile and her hands in the air like she's conducting a chorus of angels and they sound so good she's dropped her baton?"

I faced the second canvas dead on. White light bounced off white material, and this is what I told Xavier and Allegra: "This is a white canvas. There isn't a single gap in the white, it's forceful in its very flatness, so how can Ava be layered on top with this downright exuberant finger-painted effect, playing an invisible theremin . . ."

Xavier made a confounded, delighted clucking sound in the back of his throat. He took a photo of each of the blank canvases, and Allegra and I leaned over his phone as he zoomed in and zoomed out again. The white got grittier when he zoomed in, but that was all.

"Yeah," Allegra said. "I wish I'd asked Přem how he made these paint-less paintings. I think I held back because I thought I wouldn't understand visual artist chat. Now I know I should've insisted he give me a term or something I could research. Because being left behind with works like this makes me wonder who he really was. Mind you, I didn't wonder when I was with him. I felt like I just knew. This is a bloke I went to galleries and fashion shows with, and there'd be a stir when he showed up, like, *Oh, it's Přem . . . finally.* He didn't really do nights out, and he wasn't on social media, but maybe he set out to perform some of its functions? On a day out we'd stop in at ten or eleven places before he went home. It was kind of like a culture crawl . . . he'd describe everyone he introduced me to as a beautiful mind. In a way he was too much of a super connector and hyperactive man about town to get caught on camera, d'you know what I mean? I'm getting sad that I keep saying 'was.' At least the paintings are a good likeness."

She had some photos of the elder Stojaspal in good health. Karel at the beach, laughing with his feet buried in the surf. Karel in a sound studio with headphones on and pen in hand, taking notes on what he heard. Karel and Ava with forks crossed, fighting for the last meatball in a pasta bowl. She held her phone up against Karel's side of the father-son portrait and put the painter's representational accuracy beyond doubt.

There was a commotion at the doorway that connected the gallery carriage to the postal-sorting carriage; Allegra's hand tightened on my arm while Xavier went to see what was happening. He came back with Laura, two chairs, and many exclamations.

"Laura De Souza," he said, to me, to Laura, to the air. "What . . . why . . . how are the two of us travelling together again?"

Laura set down her own two chairs and gestured to us to sit. She had a folder tucked under her arm. "That's what I'm wondering. What could he possibly be doing here, the little train schoolboy all grown up? Ordinarily I'd be happy to see you, but we really can't have disruptions right now, and disruption does seem to travel with you, I'm sorry to say."

"We doubt the reunion is a coincidence," Allegra said, as she handed out round lollipops. We all took one.

Xavier and Laura spoke in French for a while. I caught "*ton père*" and "Limoges," and Laura beamed momentarily before returning to English:

"Listen, gentlemen, before we start the train up again, we need to show you something. And if there's anything you need to tell us afterwards, please come clean."

Laura looked at Allegra, to see if she had anything to add. Allegra only shrugged, so Laura took a photocopied document out of her folder and handed it to Xavier, who drew his chair closer to mine so that I could read along with him. It was the Last Will and Testament of Karel Stojaspal as filed on August 31, 2014. The name of the executor was unfamiliar, but Ava Kapoor was the sole beneficiary—*for her kindness to my son*, he'd written. And her inheritance of his property, investment portfolio, status as musical copyright beneficiary, everything, was dependent on her undergoing a psychiatric evaluation that confirmed her as being of wholly sound mind on her thirtieth birthday. Should that condition not be met, half of the proceeds of Karel Stojaspal's estate were earmarked for such medical treatments as Ava Kapoor might require for the rest of her life, and the other half would go to the institutions that had moulded him: the Prague Conservatory and the Royal Academy of Music.

For her kindness to my son . . . the son not mentioned by name. Whenever it felt like I was about to make an outburst, I silenced myself with my lollipop.

Laura leaned forward, hands on her knees, gaze like a drill, going from Xavier to me, then back to Xavier. "Guys, help us out here. Just under five years ago, after the reading of this will, Ms. Yu over there managed to convince Ava Kapoor that living together on this train would be the best way of making sure she could meet the sanity requirement."

"Such a sinister condition to make," Allegra said slowly. "Almost like a threat. Ava doesn't have any kind of psychiatric record. There's just some sort of even keel she's on. When she's moody, it's moderately moody. She did take it really hard when her dad died—they were so close. But the grief didn't drag her downstream. I think she was ready to go, but whatever it is that grounds her wouldn't budge. So after a while she went, *Ugh, I'll just have to stay here with you lot, then.* Karel was around for all of that, but maybe he was thinking the worst of the grief would hit later, or that it would all just build up? I can't work out why else he'd do this. Cut Přem out altogether and arrange the rest the way he did. But that's how it happened, so the next steps were up to us. We put our heads together and drew up a list of factors that heighten vulnerability. So we'd know what to avoid until Ava's thirtieth. I promised her four years and eight months in which she wouldn't be hungry or lonely or paralysed by finances, wouldn't have too much or too little to see, learn, and do. I promised she'd get to work on her train and get to share it, let strangers enjoy it without having to have anxiety-ridden conversations with them . . . because somewhere along the line we realised that communication was the thing we really had to address. We had to limit it. Talking to strangers can be riskier than it is rewarding; even people who know each other well talk at cross purposes and derange each other's perceptions."

"Sanity and consistency of perception are the same thing?" Xavier asked.

He'd struck a point on which they were unanimous: Laura said, "Of course it is," and Allegra said, "Yes!"

". . . And with all those precautions in place, at the end of those four years and eight months . . . payday," I said.

Allegra gave me a very slight wink. "It should've been simple. And it might still be. Wednesday's the big day. We'll all have to have some champagne together before we drop you off in Boughton."

Laura began to speak but trailed off as a sound that had been in the distance for a while now made itself distinct from the hub-bub of maintenance team conversation outside. A pitch perfect rendition of the Beach Boys' "Don't Worry Baby." It wasn't louder than the other voices calling out to each other, but it was the kind of sub-sound you wanted to shake out of your head. The whistler moved along the side of the train, and the song isolated itself within the ear, quivering just above the white noise you hear when you try to listen to your own pulse.

Then, without a break in the whistling, *Bang, bang, bang,* the carriage wall jumped.

Bang—Přem's self-portrait skipped up the wall and clattered back down. *Don't worry, baby* . . .

The four of us scattered, swearing our heads off. Xavier followed Laura back into the postal-sorting carriage while I followed Allegra into a dormitory carriage that was mostly navy blue linen and bunk beds. Allegra pressed walkie-talkie controls in what seemed like an arbitrary sequence, and we all but squashed our noses against the carriage windows as we sought out the best view of the ground directly in front of the gallery carriage. There was a fire extinguisher rolling around beside the track, and two members of the maintenance team sprinted our way and retrieved it. Allegra's walkie-talkie connected her to several crackly voices; she reeled off names and questions, but the replies were more or less the same: it had been so quick nobody had seen anything. One of the walkie-talkie voices, belonging to someone named Eric, was able to confirm that the fire extinguisher was empty, but that was all the information he had. Everybody was of the opinion that we should get moving again as soon as possible. Allegra assured them we'd be off in half an hour, tops.

When we returned to the gallery car, the wall was still again. Xavier and Laura were already seated and wearing matching expressions. They'd settled on belligerent relaxation.

"What was that . . . ?! Any ideas?"

Xavier spread his hands, and Laura shook her head. Allegra sat down too, punching in one more walkie-talkie code that linked her to Ava.

"Everything OK, beb? Over."

Ava answered with her mouth too close to the microphone;

the syllables hissed themselves into gravel, and we didn't catch what she said. But we did hear a snatch of theremin music a moment later; we might've found her song choice witty and reassuring if we hadn't just heard it whistled a few seconds ago.

Allegra said: "Ava, I'm coming over. Over!"

There was more hissing, then a laugh came through. "Allegra, I'm just practising . . . Did it sound that bad? Let me have some time to tinker with it. Over."

Laura grabbed the walkie-talkie. "It . . . wasn't bad, Ms. Kapoor. You don't worry either; practice to your heart's content. Over and out."

Allegra stood up, sat down, then stood up again and circled our chairs, chewing her nails. Laura closed the channel, stuck the device in the pocket of her jeans, and said to Xavier and me: "Wednesday is indeed the big day. And the doctor's boarding the train tomorrow to make the assessment that has to be submitted to the executor. We need a calm and quiet atmosphere. No more pulling the emergency cord for no discoverable reason."

To the carriage wall she said: "And no more whistling and fire extinguishers!"

She put a hand over her own heart for a second before continuing. "Ms. Kapoor has spoken with Dr. Zachariah weekly ever since she took up residence here, and the doctor jokes—at least I hope it is a joke—that Ms. Kapoor maintains sanity to an abnormal degree. But we can't rest on our laurels yet. The problem is that four years, seven months, and twenty days of the best laid plans can come to absolutely nothing over the course of twenty-four hours."

"Ah. Er . . . it's true that complacency's no good," Xavier said, "but it really doesn't seem like you have to do any more than you already have. We'll just stay out of everybody's way until we're home. Believe us, we have no disruptive intentions."

Laura asked: "Are you sure?" at almost exactly the same moment Allegra did. Laughing nervously, each gestured for the other to elaborate first.

"It's just that ever since you two joined us, Ms. Kapoor has been . . . skittish," Laura said.

Allegra smiled. "Maybe in your opinion, Ms. De Souza. Let's see what the qualified and experienced psychiatrist says."

"Ms. Yu . . . are you forgetting that we're back to the songs for Prěm again, from midnight 'til five? That one song in particular . . . the one that sounds like part of a soundtrack for a TV special on abusive relationships. If Dr. Zachariah observes all that and still decides Ms. Kapoor's doing well, then we'll need to find a more credible assessor pronto."

"Just out of curiosity," Allegra said, "I know we aren't friends and you're just here for work, but have you left the neutral observer zone, Ms. De Souza? Are you actively hoping that Dr. Zachariah won't confirm Ava to be of sound mind?"

Laura twirled her lollipop around inside her mouth while she thought about this.

"No," she said. "Over the years I've become biased in the other direction. I hope Ms. Kapoor does inherit. I think she would make the money behave correctly. And I like you, Ms. Yu. I know that left to your own devices you would have used these years to write music instead of chauffeuring your girlfriend around by train."

"I've been doing both without too many issues, thanks," Allegra said stiffly.

"But you are not happy with the music you write nowadays. You compare it to what you were doing before, and it is the same, almost exactly the same . . . you are unable to add anything or to blend anything in. Well, you made that choice of your own free will, so I won't embarrass you anymore. I'm telling you I like the way you have been keeping the terrifying promises you made to Ava Kapoor. I'm telling you this even though it's unprofessional to do so, since it's true that I'm not here to like anybody."

To Xavier and me, Laura said: "I shouldn't get attached. The money situation is quite serious. Ms. Kapoor has borrowed quite a lot of money on her inheritance expectations. Money to live off, and money for the work she's doing on the train . . ."

"There are companies that would lend that much based on this?" Xavier asked, raising and dropping the photocopied will.

"Ruthless ones," Laura said, and Allegra added: "With cutthroat interest rates."

Laura shrugged. "*Et voilà*, I travel with them, I send reports to my boss in Hong Kong. In theory I assist with keeping Ms. Kapoor on an even keel because that is the best way to guarantee my boss gets his money back, but it makes me feel like we're on some sort of sanitarium train, humouring the patient. So whatever, I don't hasten to dampen Ms. Kapoor's spirits when she laughs loudly, unlike some . . ."

"I think I see," I said, before Allegra could return the volley.

"So do I," Xavier said. "Sorry if we've somehow made Ava skittish."

Allegra repeated that we hadn't done that, but Laura listed the various passengers they'd picked up and dropped off over the years. Xavier and I were the thirteenth pair of honeymooners . . .

I waited for Xavier's interjection that we hadn't actually got married. He delivered as expected. We're both curious about his unerring pursuit of transparency there. (He says he doesn't quite understand it himself.) Maybe some part of Xavier Shin savours the uncomfortable pause as the other person tries to decide what to ask or say, not ask or not say. For my part, I'd argue that a pinch of unexpected information might well make otherwise formulaic exchanges more real, but in this case the outcome tends towards more awkwardness than there needs to be . . .

Anyway, I'm not saying I dislike it. Xavier's brief and obstinate amendments remind me of all the trouble we two took to discover our intentions towards each other. In the absence of progeny, or a belief that subjecting each other to a legal and economic contract guarantees us anything we really need from each other, what was the simplest and strongest sign of our bond? After all the hinting and the ranting and the silences both gentle and fearsome, what a relief it was to discover that, in the case of X and O, all it comes down to is being known by the same name. Even if that is an overestimation of our ability to keep up with whatever shenanigans life has in store for us . . .

Laura raised an eyebrow. "So this isn't a honeymoon to you?"

The question was directed at me, along with an unimpressed stare. Allegra duplicated the stare. It looked as if they'd made up their minds which Shin was the commitment-phobe who'd thrown his spanner into the honeymoon works.

"We're calling it a non-honeymoon honeymoon," I said, in my firmest, most upbeat, and hopefully image-rehabilitating voice.

Laura shrugged and continued her discourse on passengers. Couples usually weren't a bother, though more than once she'd questioned the wisdom of allowing certain other parties onboard. Most recently she'd looked askance at the thirteen exorcists of assorted denominations and belief systems who had all been summoned to a single address in Morpeth, Northumberland. ". . . And I said to Allegra, is this a train or a Tower of Babel?" But even that hadn't been a problem; Ava hadn't seemed at all unsettled and had particularly relished the notes and drawings they'd left in *The Lucky Day*'s guestbook. No spooky serenades, until us.

"Ms. De Souza's the skittish one," Allegra said. "I am too, these days."

"Because of him . . . Karel's son?" I asked. "He didn't contest the will?"

"No, he didn't. By the time the will was read, we hadn't seen or heard from him for months. Karel's mate Zeinab, the executor, says Přem knew about the will and that he really, really, really wasn't happy about it. Half of me reckons that if Přem was alive, he'd have contested the will, or at least attended Karel's funeral. The other half of me reckons Přem would wait until Ava was within spitting distance of the inheritance and then spit all over us."

Allegra crouched down between our two chairs, Xavier's and mine. She took my left hand, and she took Xavier's right hand. "Otto and Xavier Shin, I have no way of telling whether either of you are lying. You could be a pair of brilliant actors with those all-this-is-completely-new-to-me looks on your faces. And I've put such a strange bubble around the three of us, Ava, Laura, and me, that I don't know if we're going to be able to live in the real world again after this. But please. Before we get going again, I need you to either swear to me that you have nothing to do with Přemysl Stojaspal, or just take your stuff and get off the train right now."

Laura beamed at us. "If you stay, and you do anything else that might bother Ms. Kapoor, you boys will be locked up in our holding cell."

Xavier and I crunched our lollipops as we took this in. It was too Good Cop, Bad Cop for words.

"I swear we don't have anything to do with—er—him," I said. "We'll go along with you quietly from now on. Let's not keep that doctor waiting . . ."

I punctuated all this with reassuring nods, and Allegra nodded each time I did. Still holding Allegra's hand, Xavier told her the bubble she'd been building wasn't that much stranger than life in the real world.

"For instance," he said, "I know a guy who only claims to know how to say 'hello,' 'goodbye,' 'thank you,' and the days of the week in Czech. But in his sleep, he's fluent."

"What kind of things does he say?" Laura asked.

"It's sort of a cascade, really. But there is one recurring chant. *'Pojd' blíž . . . pojd' blíž . . .'*"

"What's that in English? Do you know?" I asked, somehow. Not sure how, what with my mouth having dried up all of a sudden.

Xavier leaned his shoulder against mine for a moment. "I checked. It means 'Come closer.'"

"And do you—I mean, did you? Go closer?"

"Yeah," Xavier said, "but he'd elbow me out of the bed. It wasn't me he was talking to. Anyway, we'll be out of your way now."

The whistling began again as we were leaving. I looked back at Laura, who was saying, "No . . . no, no no no," as she glanced at the wall, then at the floor. The whistler couldn't really have stretched out full length between the train and the track, couldn't be pushing the notes up out of their lungs and through the floor beneath us, but that's exactly what it sounded like. *Don't worry, baby . . .*

Xavier was already back in the postal-sorting carriage. He looked at me over his shoulder. "Aren't you going to do something about this?"

Don't worry, baby . . .

Behind us Laura and Allegra stomped on the linoleum, Allegra's trainers sparkling as she raised thunder.

"You try if you want," I said, shaking my head and brushing past him. He grabbed my arm and pushed me back into the gallery car, so hard I almost lost my footing. "Sort this out, Otto," he said.

The connecting door closed, and I pressed the button to open it again. The lightbulb rocked back and forth, splashing shadows across the walls of the gallery car. Xavier stood in full sunlight, resting his elbow on the corner of a wooden letterbox, and he won our staring match easily.

He didn't repeat himself—not aloud, anyway, but I still muttered, "As you command . . ."

Don't worry, baby . . .

Just the chorus, and the whistler was giving it everything they had.

"Don't go anywhere," I said. He said he wouldn't, the door closed again, and I turned back to Laura and Allegra. They were beside themselves with baffled fury, but their stomping had become rhythmic. I suppose that's what happens when you keep it up long enough . . . rage turns into a soft-shoe shuffle. I walked around them, calling their names until they looked at me, then, locking eyes with Allegra first, I held my right hand up, my index finger touching my thumb, and I began to whistle in time with our unseen entertainer, in a lower note so that a harmony sounded through the carriage. As below, so above. Allegra was much better at whistling than I was, so it was a relief when, after about three seconds, during which she looked more likely to burst into tears than give in and be mesmerized, she took up the notes and ran with them.

Don't worry, baby . . .

When I broke eye contact, she lifted her gaze to the blank canvas that we said we'd seen Ava in. Laura took longer to enlist. About fifteen seconds. She was badly off-key, but dedicated.

I'd guessed that the whistler was more of a soloist than an ensemble player, and he proved me right by abruptly dropping out once we'd whistled our way through one more chorus.

Don't worry, baby . . .

I never have anything up my sleeve except for the utterly

fraudulent authority with which I assure you—yes, you—that you'll get through this, whatever it is, and everything will be better. We both know nothing's all right, but when I tell you it will be, you take it. If you don't, it's because you're holding out for another outcome altogether.

9.

The train was in motion again by the time we reached our living quarters (going by the tannoy announcement it sounded as if Laura was in the driver's seat for now), but we weren't 100 percent sure of Árpád and Chela's whereabouts. There was, however, a skittering of claws on metal overhead that suggested our friends were running around on the roof of the train, heading back in our direction each time they heard their names called.

"God knows what they're up to," I said. "But I trust Árpád's judgement. Let's leave them to it."

Xavier seemed dissatisfied with this, but I think we both had very clear recall of Laura's smiley assurance that we'd be made prisoners if we created any further delays. Besides, he was still playing with the photos he'd taken of the white canvases in the gallery car, zooming in and out. As he did so, he asked me: "What have they got to do with us, these people?"

I no longer had the energy to keep lying, even though I knew that lying would set us free faster than any truth would. A break for calorie consumption would give us the strength to continue denying everything, so I borrowed Allegra's "good question" remark and suggested eating before we tried to answer it. We'd eat, and then I'd ask Xavier how often I did that, chant "Come closer," and if I'd done it last night. Hopefully he'd tell me he wasn't talking about me, or that he'd only said it to take Allegra's mind off her worries. I was happy for him to tell me anything he liked, as long as it reinforced our non-involvement with the situation onboard this train.

The track looped around an expanse of pale, glossy blue. I watched for ripples, thinking it was water at first, then deciding it was ice, even though the temperature was all wrong for it. The blue stood taller and taller as we skimmed its edge, but it only became a mountain as we left it behind. A mountain of blue quartz, foliage-free and so coolly translucent that sunset and moonrise washed along its peaks in one great wave. We silently gave each other a quick pinch; it wasn't a dream. The smell of French toast drifted through from the pantry car and caressed our nostrils, and we gave each other another quick pinch. Still not a dream.

"Now this is how honeymoons are supposed to be," Xavier said, ushering me food-ward.

Ava Kapoor was at the stove, transferring our extremely late breakfast from frying pan to plate. "Hello, Shin and Shin"—she accepted a swift kiss on each cheek and one of those flowery compliments beginning *Madame, je suis ravie . . .* from Xavier—"wearing each other's clothes and looking as if you've never slept in your lives . . . I spy true romance! Please, sit, eat while it's hot. Oh, and have you seen Chela anywhere?"

I said no, Xavier said yes, I lost the second staring match of the day, then Xavier said: "I think he meant to say that Chela's with Árpád."

"Ah," Ava said. "If they've gone looking for the passenger you saw, we'd better get ready to meet him. He may be wily enough to slip through the clutches of one mongoose, but he could never evade two."

The carriage had been scrubbed and wiped clean from top to bottom, and two plates stacked with French toast were already on the table, along with the cutlery needed to eat it in a civilised fashion.

Ava brought her own plate over, wiping her hands on her apron as she sat down with us.

"He's here, isn't he?" she said, without preamble. "Přem. You've brought him, or he sent you here without you knowing it. To try to drive me mad at the last minute."

I fed a bite of French toast to Xavier and said: "I don't know what you're talking about, Ava."

Xavier picked up his own knife and fork, fed me a bite of French toast—an extra-large bite—and said: "Otto . . . you still don't seem to understand that I'm not going to let you gaslight anybody."

I choked (where was the Xavier who'd backed me up in front of Allegra, corroborating an encounter he hadn't witnessed?), and Ava poured me a glass of water while my loving partner patted me on the back.

"Aside from his natural inclination towards deforming reality, there's the fact that we've all but promised not to talk to you," Xavier told Ava.

"You were just with Allegra?"

"And Laura. They told us about your friend's will."

"The will, the will . . . that's all we're living for these days. But about those two. Something tells me that all this has been too much for them. Suppose we succeed . . . Suppose I inherit after all, and as soon as the money side of things is sorted, those other two consider their duties done and go off together without me? They've had to play to each other's strengths for an extended period of time—"

"So they respect each other," I said.

"They've never felt it necessary to treat each other like invalids—"

Xavier shrugged, and so did I.

"And they've never flirted in front of me."

"Oh." I thought about the myriad ways in which friends can be flirtatious, cheekily saluting each other from either side of established boundaries. For those two not to flirt at all, when they had to have looked at each other and thought about it . . . oh dear.

"Maybe I've got the wrong end of the stick," Ava said, sawing at her French toast. "Maybe they're just tolerating each other, or they're the kind of friends who . . . don't happen to share a sense of humour? What did you think? Did it seem as if there might be something else between them?"

Xavier nodded, and after a couple of gulps of water I concurred. With great unease. Xavier might have thought I wanted to gaslight Ava, but I thought he was overestimating her ability to handle changes that might not be to her liking after an epoch of changes more or less handpicked to keep her happy.

Ava drizzled more maple syrup onto her toast; her hand trembled slightly, but all she said was: "It's good to get an outside opinion."

"Ava." I fed her a bite of French toast too. "We're only saying it's not impossible. On the other hand, they seem fond of you. As far as we can tell, anyway."

She scrunched up her face and dropped her fork onto her plate. "What is this superior feeding method that makes the French toast taste better? Do it again."

I did, and Xavier asked her: "So did you really mean it when you told people you couldn't see Přem, or what?"

Ava chewed, nervously and for a long time. She drank some water.

"The Přem question is the one that decides whether I inherit," she said. "But I don't know which answer is the one that confirms sanity. I'm not talking about the answer that satisfies Karel's requirement, or Dr. Zachariah's, but the one that satisfies mine."

She accepted another bite of French toast, then stood, talking with her mouth full. "I'd better go. I've left a file in the bread bin . . . Laura and Allegra would never look in there. Read it and . . . add to it for me, OK?"

Her walkie-talkie buzzed in her apron pocket as she hurried away.

10.

What we found in the bread bin: a folder with the name *Přemysl Stojaspal* (in Ava's handwriting). Inside, a sheaf of handwritten texts, each in a different hand, with a typed table of contents on top—names matched to page numbers.

Ava Kapoor
Allegra Yu
Laura De Souza
Zeinab Rashid

Beneath these names, Ava had written

Otto Shin
Xavier Shin

I flipped through the sheaf of handwritten texts looking for the entries pertaining to us, but Xavier said: "We're meant to add to it ourselves. She wants it in writing . . . what we know about him."

"What are you saying? You know about this guy?"

"I'm not sure yet," he said. "But maybe, once we've looked at the rest . . ."

"People often don't realise what they know," I said, quoting one of my favourite books, *"and only when it is explicitly stated does it become obvious to them.* Something like that?"

He answered me with a kiss that counselled the wisdom of speaking to him in Ludvík Vaculík quotations, and we took the file back to Clock Carriage, where we read the accounts in order.

11.

AVA KAPOOR

I used to busk in what I think of as Newcastle's town centre, Old Eldon Square. I'd get there early in the morning, set up my instrument, and start playing as the sun came up. I played facing the east, with St. George slaying his dragon behind me. Though really it is less of a killing happening atop that pedestal and more a depiction of some fascination—a courtship, possibly—between the saint and the serpent. George courteously offers the dragon a metal spike, the dragon just as gallantly ingests it, and both seem gratified that it's going down so well. I played theremin-adapted reveilles until the shops opened, and when you do that, passersby really give you whatever they have to give. Sniggers and stares. Comments about noise pollution. Phone numbers. Doughnuts. Song requests. Applause. Impromptu dance routines. Spare change. A five-pound note "'cause I'm not sure exactly what you're up to but it's a ballsy move; girls like you remind me I wouldn't want to live in any other city" . . .

I played for an hour and a half regardless. Then I'd go to work: online customer service for a few different companies, just me and my laptop logged into a few different company e-mail accounts, with a number of databases open so I could check the typical things customers enquire and complain about or contact somebody who could find out what was what. Phone calls were rare during the day, and I liked that because it meant I'd be able to answer immediately if there was anything about my dad.

In short: it was the standard life of a music scholar who'd love to play vocationally but can't. Time, money, talent, and grit—I think I'd have been able to do more with my theremin if I'd been lacking only two of those four essentials. But I lacked all four. And what did I have instead? Realism. What a gift! Most of the time it's as if my life is hiding from me, but as I play, note by note, I echolocate it.

One morning in Eldon Square, the most beautiful emergency I'd ever seen walked by, dressed in red from head to toe and chugging a can of Red Bull. She had her earphones in, but she pulled them out and listened to my playing. She didn't stop walking, and I had to choose between looking at her and following the notation on the sheets in front of me, so I lost her. But she came by again the next day, and the next—each time dressed as if she was going somewhere special, or as if that day was a very important day. But when we spoke, she'd tell me she'd just come from picking up or dropping off packages and dry cleaning and things like that. And her name was Allegra Yu.

One morning she asked if I was OK with her recording my busking. I said I was, but that I didn't want her to put it online or anything. She told me she needed the recording so that she could compose for me. Compose for me!

I didn't see her for a couple of weeks; then she came and gave me what she'd written: an untitled, spinning-top sort of sonata that slowed down into an arch, darting, aching minuet. I was a bit scared to play it in public and wondered if that was how Prince had felt about performing sometimes. It felt like people might get pregnant just from listening to this. Men, women, everybody . . .

The "raunchy spaceship" song went down well, and over the following weeks Allegra Yu wrote me two more songs. The second song was a boozy, bluesy piece that made my theremin sound as if it was looking back on a long life of crime, and the third song was a dance tune that had all these charming little trips and falls in it, just like a row of dizzy ducklings. After the third song, realising that we'd already danced together and slept together and aided and abetted each other, I asked her out. She said I'd had her kicking her blankets at night, wondering if she was no longer a genius. "Usually it only takes one song . . ."

I brought her aboard my train, "The Lucky Day," for a picnic dinner; I'd prepared all the food myself so we ended up sticking with wine. We lit candles, and even though I'd dusted that particular carriage just hours before, I saw that the dust helixes were back, in enhanced definition, as if determined to stop us from romanticising this evening on a broken-down train that hadn't gone anywhere for over forty years. She announced that a smugglers' train is never what it seems to be, blew the candles out again, and lay her head on my lap.

"OK . . . where are we going? Announce the stations," she said.

That was my moment to sound well-travelled, or an imaginative match for her, but I had a lapful of runway model and couldn't think, couldn't think . . . yet I had to say something . . . and at that moment the spirit of Agatha Christie took over and made me name stations from "the 4:50 from Paddington," all haphazardly: "Waverton. Haling Broadway. Barwell Heath. Change here for Roxeter and Chadmouth . . ."

She stopped me there, at Barwell Heath. We dallied at that station for quite some time, and left with love bites as souvenirs.

Empty room gig or no empty room gig, Allegra Yu is the one I play for. I've come to know her better than anyone, I think, and she me.

But there's one matter that divides us—that divides me

and everybody else who's contributed to this file: Allegra has seen and interacted with Přemysl Stojaspal—several times this has occurred in my presence—while I look where she is looking, and listen to the silence before and after the remarks she makes, and I see and hear nothing. This is not good for my relationship with Allegra, or with anybody, really . . . when Přem enters our conversation as a subject . . . or not even as a subject, if we talk about anything even vaguely linked to Přem, we begin to lie to each other. We tell ourselves we're being tactful, but it is more desperate than that. We're trying not to lose each other.

There must actually be a Přemysl Stojaspal. Everybody— and I mean everybody—behaves as if there is . . . so to me Přem exists in that sense, and sometimes also in a vaguer sense of a listener, some reaction that forms when certain notes are mixed into air. I have no personal knowledge of him otherwise.

I can state that it was Allegra who introduced me to him, or at least, to his father. Allegra was Karel's personal assistant and was supposed to be organizing the logistics of life so he had more time for his own projects. But he was all, "Oh, Allegra, if I was thirty years younger," and she was all, "Mate . . . if you were thirty years younger I'd still be gay." I'm the one Karel's (conditionally) made sole beneficiary of his will, but Allegra's the one who'd get phone calls from him at all hours of the day. "Hang up and don't answer: I want to leave you voicemail," he'd say, and fill her voicemail inbox with musings only she could decipher and the occasional blast of music so she'd "see what he meant."

Karel's son was somewhere in his thirties and lived with his dad. I'm not flagging that up as unusual—I'd be one to talk, since I was still living with mine. I had love reasons and health reasons as well as economic reasons for that, but I did pick up some subtext that Karel's son was living with him mainly for health reasons. The son's, not Karel's.

My understanding of Přem's condition was that he couldn't be alone at night. That's what Karel told me, without going into what was meant by "couldn't." From a very early age Přemysl got <u>bad</u> at night. Agitated, wouldn't sleep, would get violent, other things. Karel did once tell me that Přemysl took especial issue with him, Karel, sleeping. <u>He simply wouldn't stand for it.</u> Karel Stojaspal told me that as a boy Přemysl conceived a notion that he'd disappear unless somebody kept thinking about him, and that Karel and his wife had indulged that fancy until it had grown to <u>unmanageable proportions</u>. Medication didn't work, therapy had worked for a while, but he tended to run through therapists <u>like a swarm of termites through floorboards</u> . . . (Karel's terms underlined. He was very tired when he made that termite comparison, but it sticks with me as I've never heard anyone talk about their own child like that.)

A few months into our acquaintance, Karel stopped discussing Přemysl with me, and only reluctantly mentioned him. That was partly my fault. I just didn't know how to look at him while he talked about his invisible son. We went through the stage where I'd laugh or smile; then the stage where I tried to treat it all as a sort of philosophical riddle; the phase where I got angry with Karel; the fearful phase, which still comes and goes. I almost had a panic attack when Karel gave me the paintings, quite publicly, at a restaurant lunch he held for my twenty-second birthday, with an empty seat at the table beside me. A seat our friends addressed as Přem, though from time to time they'd joke and laugh with different fissures in the space all around me, and those fissures were also Přem Stojaspal. How they all admired the self-portrait . . . though he'd lost all that weight, so it wasn't quite as accurate now, hahaha! I honestly couldn't breathe at all. I couldn't really look at the paintings for a few days, and when I did, I studied that face that our friends apparently recognized, and I considered moving to a different city, breaking up with Allegra, and getting new friends who'd never heard of the Stojaspals. But . . . abandoning Allegra and our people, the loveliest loves of both our lives, just because of some guy? As if.

It was OK when I was with Karel or the others and Přem didn't join us—increasingly he didn't bother, I'm told. "He loves you but has received your message of hate," is how one friend put it. Of course I didn't hate Přem (how could I?), but I made things worse when I tried to play along. One of the only times I've seen Karel look as sick as I felt at that birthday lunch was when I tried greeting him and Přemysl simultaneously one evening. Přemysl hadn't yet arrived. Karel laughed, though he could tell I hadn't been joking.

Then he threw me out of his house and told me never to come back. He repented after what I'm guessing was one of the "bad" nights with Přem; Allegra played go between . . .

It was fine when I played at night, and it was, supposedly, just the two of us. Me and Přem. Don't think I didn't try to catch sight of him in mirrors and in glass—I was ready to believe he was a spirit, anything. But it was an empty room.

However, some things I remember Karel telling me before Přem became a taboo topic between us: When Přem had been younger there'd been games that used to amuse him through the night. But once he reached the age of putting away childish things, the nights were the worst ever. But he'd have good nights if Karel played for him all night. That worked for a while, but between theremin playing all night and sleeping all day, Karel was in a bad way and not really able to take part in his own existence. Concerned friends volunteered to play for Přem at night, and even drew up a roster, but Karel only wanted them to know the personable, multitalented daytime Přem who did his father so much credit. He also didn't think they'd take the task seriously enough; they'd fall asleep, and then doom would befall. Or something.

Allegra played for Přem herself—for seven nights, by her count. She stayed wide awake, but so did he. Bitching about her playing until dawn, she told me. Přem kept saying she should stick to composing, even though he could hardly say her compositions had more substance. Allegra asked me if I agreed with him . . . if I thought Karel agreed with him, etc. . . . Přemysl being mean to her throughout the night got a ruminative wheel turning, and I hoped and hoped Karel would get someone else to play for this Přemysl before Allegra broke herself on that groundless wheel. I remember she was on antidepressants at the time, but I've noticed that the cushion those pills can provide isn't that thick.

Then I needed money even more than ever, and Allegra handed her nighttime theremin playing position over to me. The first night I went, I meant to have it out with this Přemysl, but Karel showed me into an empty bedroom. He didn't speak to the room . . . Sometimes I hold on to that as evidence of something, I don't know what, but that first night Karel didn't speak to the room . . . just told me to play as discussed, and left me to it. If the setup was exactly the same with me as it was with Allegra, that would mean Přem Stojaspal would've been there in the bed the whole night, talking shit about my theremin playing while I played my heart out without letting a word pass my lips. If . . . *if* that's what happened, did that . . . make him happy somehow? Help him sleep? Karel seemed amazed when he looked in at us just before dawn. He said I was a miracle worker. I thought he was just an effusive man.

Two more things:

One night, the very first night I didn't bother to check

the room before I began playing, there was someone in Přem Stojaspal's bed. She sat up among the pillows, all "hand me a glow stick and let's rave!" as soon as I started playing one of Allegra's songs—the giddy duckling dance, as it happens. It was Chela. Chela Kapoor, a mongoose who deserves all the finer things in life, and often gets them, I'm sure. I played Allegra's song twice more for her, and then she gave what must be the mongoose equivalent of a sigh and left the room. I actually stopped playing for about half an hour when she left. I thought about going to look for her, I thought maybe the mongoose was Přem, that what Karel hadn't wanted to mention was that Přem turned into a mongoose at night . . . I thought all sorts of things, but I was unable to reconcile any of it with the previous nights. She was a very friendly manifestation I mustn't allow to distract me from what I was there to do. So I resumed the usual program. Hoping all the while that she'd come back. She didn't return to the bedroom, but when I was leaving the house, she gave Karel's flower beds a good trampling as she pursued me to the garden gate. I phoned Karel to ask if it was OK for the mongoose to come home with me, and Karel, sounding very surprised, said that was up to Přem. "She's his mongoose. Her name is Chela."

To me this was like saying, "That's Tinkerbell's mongoose . . . look out . . . Tink might get angry with you!" I took Chela home without further ado. Dad was at first inclined to treat her as a hallucination brought on by his pain medication but very soon warmed to her, and we've been the best of friends ever since.

The second thing: this is my ruminative wheel, like the one Allegra might have broken herself on if she'd spent many more nights playing for Přem. Is there anything I could have done that would have made it so that Karel Stojaspal could be alive and well today?

Karel had cysts on his kidneys. He knew something was wrong for quite a long time—we'll never know how long— but he didn't seek treatment until he collapsed at a meeting, was taken to hospital, and a scan revealed the extent of the damage. Karel had to have a transplant. He had to, and naturally, his son, Přemysl, was the donor.

Naturally. Tests had been run, compatibility was assured, Karel didn't want to die, he still had a project he wanted— needed—to complete, and he would. Přem, he told me, was more than willing, was all but ready to rip the kidney out and hand it over himself. The date of the operation was arranged.

I was dazed, couldn't believe he meant to go ahead with this thing. Karel wanted to try to live with Přem's kidney in his body? *Přem's?* A non-corporeal kidney? I wrote the date of the operation down, and I took it as many holy places as I could reach with my railcard over the course of five days. Temples, a synagogue, a church, a woodland glade, a shrine by the sea. I believe in some greater power, but not formally. I don't know how to pray; maybe I'm as blind and deaf to the greater power as I was to Přem's presence. In the holy places I asked what would happen on the date I'd written down; I asked if there was any way Karel was going to survive. I asked the power to move that ludicrously stubborn man, to make him seek another donor, try something, anything, else. Answers came, but that thing you read and hear about, that thing that happens to people when they try to access some exterior truth and sink so deep that they don't recognize the voice they hear . . . it wasn't like that for me. I always heard the answers in my own voice. Shallow consciousness problems.

I went back to Karel, and we had one more fight, one more terrible fight about Přem. And everything I said was wrong. I tried to force Karel to say he didn't have a son; Karel tried to force me to admit that I am playing some minx-like game of influence, trying to drive his son to lunacy just because. Apparently Přem was there, shouting that I should be ashamed. But Allegra says she was with Přem that afternoon, so the bit about Přem shouting was probably Karel fighting me.

The operation went ahead the following week. Five months passed, and Karel was alive. I didn't visit him, he didn't want to see me, but I went back to all the holy places and kissed the earth, kissed the stones, kissed whatever I could kiss for the gladness of being wrong. In the sixth month, Karel got really sick. His body had rejected Přem's kidney. The medication he was taking was supposed to safeguard against that, but I don't think anyone can imagine what kind of charge Karel's medication was trying to take on. It failed. Then there was the funeral, and then there was the reading of the will, and the wheel of thought as I turn words over. The words I said to Karel Stojaspal about his son. I said it all wrong. But the right words—what are they?

12.

ALLEGRA YU

Ava,

Přem asked me how I can trust you. He wasn't talking about your behaviour towards him; he was really sad about Chela. He couldn't get over her. "Ava Kapoor . . . Ava Kapoor . . . that girl stole my fucking mongoose!" Karel and I looked into getting him another mongoose, but he said no one could take Chela's place, that one day Chela would realise she'd made a mistake and come back to him; he was basically a spoken-word country and western ballad. To Přem Stojaspal, you will always be the girl who stole his mongoose.

Well, not only that. According to Přem, a charismatic performer is, fundamentally, a manipulator. Nothing more, nothing less. You play and it brings Přem rest, you play and I

lose my heart to you, you play and Chela realises it's time for
a companion upgrade. Přem informs me you'll never stop
because all you want is to find out what effect you can have.
Don't get bigheaded: He didn't talk about you much. But
when he did, it sounded like he'd given you a lot of thought.
You and your ways.

I think Přem had a crush on you. Unclear what kind: he
was celibate, as far as I knew. Admirers sent him bouquets,
and he'd set the flowers upright in jugs full of pear brandy,
saying that flowers need to have a good time too. I still hear
from people who thought I was his girlfriend; possibly
because he told them so. And I did act quite girlfriend-y.
Picking out his signature scent and buying him silk ties and
things like that. But I only bought the tie because it looked
like it was made for him. And it was on sale . . . and I was
interested in Přem's look because he was like me—operating
on this borderline of attractiveness where clothes and
accessories make all the difference. It's not something you
could understand, Ms. Stunner in a Shapeless Shift Dress.

You might want to know how Přem behaved around
you. In the early days of you ignoring him, he'd follow you
around the room with heavy objects, pretending he was
about to brain you with them. Glass ashtrays, chunky vases.
We didn't smile at those antics even when we wanted to.
There could have been an accident if we encouraged him to
keep that nonsense up. But it was several different kinds of
funny, Přem waving barbecue tongs over your head at

Karel's garden party as you stood there sipping Pimm's and lemonade and talking quite seriously with a zoologist about the fact that all living organisms do is let each other down. I think the zoologist had told you that only female mosquitoes bite—that they do it because the protein and iron in our blood helps their eggs develop. And you were all disappointed. "They shouldn't bite other females . . . we're meant to stick together . . ." The zoologist said that if you insisted on affiliating with female mosquitoes, then surely sacrificing your health was a way of sticking together. But you said you didn't want to sacrifice your health! "And so the cycle of letting each other down goes on," you wailed. "I'm sorry, mosquito mothers. I'm so sorry, I know you're only biting me for the sake of your babies, but I can't give up my blood and get sick for them . . ." It was hard to tell whether the zoologist realised you'd just had one cocktail too many, but I think Přem did. He'd already nudged me closer to you by the time you started to hiccup and sway. You put your head on my shoulder, and he gave up the tong pantomime and went off to grill some more meat. Thinking about his subsequent behaviour around you, the keyword is "shy." I remember maybe four other gatherings all three of us were at. Přem stayed out of your way and didn't speak to you directly. But he made sure he was able to hear what you were saying. And every now and then he'd turn towards you, with a semi-irritated but mostly hopeful smile, ready for the moment when you accidentally made eye contact with him.

He was one of those extroverted introverts . . . he was at home a lot, reading and taking care of his dad's publishing house—keeping that going seemed to mean a lot to him. But twice a week, maybe three times if there were a lot of people to see, he'd be out and about. I'd go too, when I could, or I'd hear about some doings of his. He might have had a drinking problem? It was hard to tell. "Never too early for beer" was a motto of his, and he'd drink like a fish all day but still be steady on his feet and as cogent as you please. But, Ava, you remember how we were semi-sure Karel was teetotal? We never saw him touch a drink, but I saw him blind drunk. Přem and I would find him like that in the evening. I'd come back to the house to say hi to Karel after having watched Přem calmly put away tens of pints, and it was Karel who was completely out of it. I mean crawling around on the floor whispering in Czech, then when Přem tried to help him up he'd say things like, "You! Don't get ahead of yourself, young man! You are my creature!"

Or he'd get all melancholy and ask Přem if he happened to remember dying as a little boy. "We buried you in the forest, your mother and I . . . with a green linden leaf. The brightest we could find, so you wouldn't need a night-light. Do you remember?"

Přem would look annoyed and say, "Is there any chance you could save these jokes for another time?" And he'd haul his dad over his shoulder, take him upstairs, and put him to bed.

Is being an only child like being the family's black sheep

and pride and joy combined? Personally, I recommend having siblings . . . as many as possible. I could have got lucky with mine, but surely it stands to reason that four brothers and two sisters make a really good buffer between you and a bunch of parental hopes and expectations. You also give and get a lot of love in a fairly relaxed, hands-off style. Since we can't really keep track of each other, we Yu sibs just make the moves we need to make and try our best to clean up after ourselves, only calling the others in as the forklift truck option when there's just too much shit to shovel. And Mum and Dad end up feeling like parenting champions who've raised seven solvent overachievers.

I know that with you and your dad it was mostly just the two of you, and you were really good mates. I'm saying that it was what I saw of Přem's home life that made me want to grab his arm and recommend siblings. Then again, if you asked me what his life really was (and that is what you're asking me, isn't it?), what his days were made up of, what he latched on to for a sense of purpose or whatever, I couldn't tell you. With Karel, at least for the last three years of his life or so, it was that novel he wanted to finish writing. The one that got edited—possibly by Přem—and published as an incomplete novella about a year after he died.

I don't know any more than you do about the wording of Karel's will. How were you kind to Přem Stojaspal? Ava, you know I say this lovingly, but you treated that man as if he was, literally, nothing.

Moving from what I don't know to what I would like to

know: About that fire in Dulwich. The day Přem destroyed
his artworks . . . what was going through his mind? Apart
from generating some pyrotechnic drama, I mean. That was
years and years of effort; some of it remarkable. I was talking
about it with Laura (De Souza) the other day, and she said,
"Maybe it was a kind of donation, just like his kidney was?"

I just looked at her, like, OK, continue. But that was it.
She looked so happy . . . "There you go, all solved!"

About Karel: I don't think it'll bother you that in my
opinion it was a one-sided love there, with all the love on
your side. You're your father's daughter that way. Enjoying
people no matter what. But it bothered me that Karel was so
two-faced, all affectionate and full of praise when you were
around and then organizing behind your back. And now I'm
catching myself saying one thing and meaning something
else. I'm speaking ill of the man who mentored me because
even though he put so much time and energy into helping
me find my own way, he thought more highly of you, your
opinions, your perceptions or whatever. That hurts. But you
should still believe me when I tell you that when it came to
testing you, Karel went to greater lengths than you realise.
He was pulling stunts he wouldn't even have bothered
thinking about if I or one of his other young satellites had
announced his very much existent son was in fact
nonexistent.

I've mentioned the gatherings the three of us were at, but
I've heard there were other gatherings where Přem was

present but everyone had to act as if he wasn't, and gatherings without Přem, where the rule was to behave as if he was there. The lunch Karel held for your birthday, for instance: Přem wasn't there. You're probably going, How would I know that when I wasn't there either? (more about that in a sec), but Přem told me so himself. Karel invited him, but Přem saw no point in another awkward couple of hours in which he tried to befriend you and got nowhere. Přem asked that his paintings be given to you as a birthday present and bowed out. But Karel said to him: "Great, I'll just have everyone act as if you're there and see what she does."

I asked Karel if that was really the plan. He said it was, and I said I wasn't going to join in. He told me it was just a prank, but I said I still wasn't going to join in and I'd be surprised if any of the others did. Then Karel said I was better off not showing up at all, that if I did, I'd get the sack and he'd employ another assistant immediately. I drafted the job advertisement for his next assistant that same afternoon, and when I gave it to him, he looked surprised—in a good way, which surprised me in turn, so we were both standing there with these "Huh!" expressions. Then he said: "So what now?"

I told him I was going to drive trains. That was the year we worked on the Lucky Day until it started to look like more than a freight train. I was down in Crewe every other weekend, sometimes with you and your dad, sometimes with

Přem and a couple of others, lugging tools and paint pots
and wheelbarrows stacked with all sorts of sheets and rolls
down to the stabling yard. Somewhere in the middle of
all that I'd applied for an apprenticeship with Arriva,
expecting them to turn me down. But as you know, they
didn't . . . and the interview was on the same day as your
birthday lunch . . .

Stop cursing me for not warning you about Karel's
prank. And stop cursing our friends. Two of them had books
under contract to Karel's publishing house and felt like they
had to dance to his tune. The others . . . I asked about it, and
it looks as if Karel gave different people different reasons for
what he wanted them to do. People thought they were
helping you, giving you a lighthearted way to admit that
you'd been uncharacteristically cruel towards Přem, stuff like
that. They thought it could be a conversation starter for the
next time the two of you saw each other. But some of our
friends didn't buy any of the reasons Karel was trying to feed
them. They only saw malice. Sonia told me Karel said to her:
"Either Ava's crazy, or we are. Don't you think we've got to
teach her a lesson?" Feuzi still says Karel decided to drive
you mad, plain and simple, and the will is the final test of
whether it worked.

Přem asked me how I can trust you, and Karel
mistrusted you outright. They both get a special hypocrisy
award for going on like that at the same time as they
depended on you and what you played for Přem at night.

I trust you, Ava. When I show you what I've done, you

greet it as whole. No concerning yourself with what's absent, or parallels you wish to hear. You listen for what is already there. You were the first person I'd met who did that for my songs. This isn't to say that I feel safe with you. Safety is something else.

That's all I know about you and me and Přem and Karel.

13.

LAURA DE SOUZA

Ms. Kapoor,

You have asked me to write down my recollections regarding Přemysl Stojaspal. In case we need to review some details, you say, without specifying what events might make this necessary. You will recall that I initially refused, but I am now complying because you've promised that if I do, you'll stop the racket you're making and let us sleep in peace.

I believe that I've seen Přemysl Stojaspal—or, at least, a man resembling the one whose portrait hangs in the gallery car of the Lucky Day—once.

I know . . . why this avoidance of clear confirmation . . . did I see him or not? Unfortunately, having to report activities onboard this train once a week has made me overly cautious. My employer values specificity over certainty.

Both Ms. Yu and I learnt to drive trains on the East
Coast Main Line, at roughly the same time, though her pace
was different from mine. We didn't cross paths back then—
this is something we've discovered through conversation. I
showed up with a Canadian high school diploma and a
robust resistance to being examined, so I wasn't able to take
Ms. Yu's university graduate fast track . . . I trained part time
whilst completing four years of railroad and rail station shift
work instead. What did I do on the station and around the
track? What didn't I do! But here's the bit you want: during
my final six months of training I landed a shift as a
conductor. I was living in Durham at the time, and the
segment of the route that I checked tickets for passed from
Durham through to Edinburgh Waverley. I'd eat something
at the other end—or sometimes stay the night, depending on
any station shifts that came back again. This was where I
saw you, Ava, and the portrait look-alike—on the
Edinburgh Waverley to Durham route. You see a lot of
things on trains, but when I look back over those six months
of train conducting, I'd say you getting on the train along
with the portrait look-alike and the sleeping mongoose was
the seventh or eighth most memorable sight. It was about
half past six in the morning. You had the mongoose all
swaddled up like a baby (fooling the sum total of zero fellow
passengers, by the way), and it looked as if you were trying to
get away from him without attracting attention to your fear.
You took a window seat and huddled up with Chela,

checking your phone every few seconds. Your companion
was wearing silk pajamas underneath a trench coat, and he
took the window seat directly behind you and stared at you,
steadily and angrily, he was all, GRRRRR, at the back of
your head. And two or three times, very hesitantly, he'd raise
a hand up over your shoulder. I think he intended to snatch
the mongoose! But then you'd cuddle her and the man
would look all gloomy. After I checked his ticket, he did ask
me whether conductors could arrest passengers in lieu of the
police. I told him I would check and asked if there was a
problem.

The man in the silk pajamas pointed at you, Ms. Kapoor,
and whispered to me that you'd just stolen his mongoose.
And he asked me what he should do. He looked as if he was
at his wit's end; I pitied him and asked if he'd tried talking
to you about it. He said yes, he'd tried and tried. I asked if I
should mediate, and he said no, no, there was nothing left to
say, that I should either detain you or leave you be. You may
indeed have stolen that mongoose, but you did not seem in
any way a threat to other passengers, so naturally, I let you
be. It was a very short trip. I checked your tickets at
Newcastle, and when I came back around at Chester-le-
Street, all three of you had gone.

The second incident I will mention is not a sighting of
Přemysl Stojaspal but a sort of postscript regarding my
change of career. I have a history of violence that renews
itself whenever I come into contact with the general public;

this is the conclusion drawn from almost every prior form of employment I've tried my hand at. There were two altercations with passengers during my time on the East Coast Main Line—one sort of blew over without any consequences, but the other was serious enough to bring about my dismissal. After the train job I worked as a nightclub bouncer for a few months, against the advice of everybody who knew me—they said I would end up in prison. And I did. It was a four-year sentence, and I got into fights while I was inside as well. Partly because I'm someone who just gets into fights, Ms. Kapoor. People piss me off with their bullshit, and I give them a smack—or vice versa. There is no point asking me why I get so angry. You should go to the people who are disrespectful until they get hit and ask them why they're like that. But partly the fighting was a little bit calculated as well. I didn't have the tolerance a person needs to be part of society, so I thought it would be for the best if I never returned to it. But it was only society I'd given up on, not life, so if I had to go, I'd have to be killed.

I don't think like that anymore. Not after these years spent unseeing the world with you and Ms. Yu. But back then, towards the end of my sentence, I'd only fought with other inmates, so the conflict instigators were hardly ever revealed. The guards couldn't pin anything on me, so on paper I was good as gold . . . and a few months before my sentence was up, I was offered opportunities to apply for jobs and start looking for housing on the outside. I wasn't interested. I got a letter congratulating me on securing a position at a loans company that would begin seven days after my release. The letter also invited me to stipulate my own monthly salary; my first month would be paid in advance to cover any expenses I'd incur getting to work. It had been sent by airmail and had a Hong Kong postmark. I hadn't applied for that job. Or any job. I threw the letter away. A couple of days later, one of the guards approached me with pen and paper, saying, "Mr. Lin's waiting . . . Write down your salary . . ."

I guess I was supposed to tremble and go, "Oh my God, this Mr. Lin has eyes and ears everywhere!" But I was still in this state of apathy unless there was a chance of a proper fight. I didn't ask any questions, just wrote down any old figure. The guard must have posted it. A few days later, Mr. Lin visited me himself, put the sheet with the numbers on it down in front of me, and said "That's a bit high. Maybe after five years . . . but let's talk about now."

He wanted me to monitor the situation regarding a loan he'd paid out. We looked at Karel's will together. The sums you'd been borrowing from Mr. Lin were getting larger and larger, but based on the size of the inheritance, he didn't mind that. What if that equilibrium of yours didn't pan out, though? Mr. Lin doesn't think Karel made that a condition just for fun. And he does think Ms. Yu's so soft that she'd just stand by going "Oh no!" while you lost your grip on reality. So it wouldn't hurt to throw in a participating observer of his own—that's what he told me.

I don't remember my reply; something about it being nice of him to care about how you were doing. I do remember that after I said whatever I said, he asked me to look at him carefully. I did. His eyes strangled light. He said, "Laura, you can see it, right? That I'm not a good person. If you make me lose money, I will eradicate you from the earth. I'm a craftsman, and I never leave the work to an inferior practitioner. I do it all myself."

Mr. Lin had a fancy smartwatch on—against visiting rules and regulations, of course. Holding his wrist beneath the table and inviting me to look down at the watch, he showed me some pictures that made it very hard for me not to throw up right there in the visiting room. He had them saved in a special photo album. He talked me through the processes depicted in a tone of humble absorption very similar to the ones you hear in art restoration video voiceovers. But he also told me he believed in consent. "I'll tell you about the job, and if you don't want to do it, you won't hear from me again. I'm here because a friend recommended you. A close friend."

I asked which friend, and he said: "Přem Stojaspal. Son of the guy whose will this is. Seems he's anxious for this Ava to inherit. That or a detailed eyewitness account of whatever disaster befalls her. He's a tricky one." Tricky Přemysl Stojaspal may well be, but I'd never met him. Or so I thought. I didn't exchange names with the man who boarded the train with you either . . . now you see why I told you I couldn't help with your enquiries. Here they are anyway, Ms. Kapoor. The notes of a former hothead who took a job based on the conviction that she'd finally met an opponent who could overpower her will to live.

14.

ZEINAB RASHID

Dear Ava,

I hope you and Allegra are pulling off that old sanity trick, all right; I think about you both often. I think about Karel, too, and Přem. I considered not writing this letter to you, and then I considered not sending it—I have a feeling this is a common reaction among those you've asked to try to put Přem in writing. In my case, there's an additional sense of impropriety. It's not right for the executor of Karel's will to gossip and speculate about his state of mind when he wrote it. Anyway, if you're reading this, I found a way to dismiss those scruples.

Karel was one of the first students to take my History of Music for Strings course, you know. And Allegra was one of the last. My first impressions of both students were so wide

of the mark I can only laugh them off. I thought Karel
needed a bit more self-confidence and Allegra needed a bit
less. They both took an interest in my lecture on an
eighteenth-century priest and an instrument he devised—a
hypothetical instrument that could not be brought into
actuality despite many years of labour. I didn't realise the
extent to which that story took hold of Karel Stojaspal's
imagination until I read "The Ocular Harpsichord"—have
you read it, Ava, the novella Karel wrote? It's all in there, in
the chilling immediacy of Karel's "I," as he tells of Louis
Bertrand Castel's proposal to make music visible to the
naked eye, and then every grain of the quicksand that drew
him into its embrace as he failed. The ruin of his health and
finances. The blighting of his view of Creation.

Allegra didn't get it. She kept looking all around her
during that lecture, seeking the point she was missing in the
expressions of the other students. But then A's viable ideas
come in clusters; if one doesn't ripen after all, there's still a
good chance one of the others will, so why get into a tizzy
over the one concept? Karel adores breezy prodigal talents.
He married one after graduation. A former classmate of his,
in fact. Poppy Dixon. I was at their wedding, and then they
moved to Newcastle once Poppy started as a 2nd Violin for
the Royal Northern Sinfonia. Poppy was a bit too nice for
Karel. No, what I mean is that Karel was too cruel for
Poppy, but never allowed her to realise it. Karel's cruel
streak, his tendency to taunt and prod, so perplexed Poppy
that he feared she wouldn't put up with it. He hid that cruel

streak from his wife and only showed it to his friends. Which was perfectly lovely for us, of course. However: I will let those stories die.

We frequently double dated when they were in town— me and Stefan, Karel and Poppy. We were just about old enough to be their parents, but we probably looked more like their grandparents. Those two had such a glow about them, and didn't yet understand about mortgages and things like that. Karel said Poppy gave him music. She'd wake up humming, and he'd be off at once, setting what he'd heard into a composition. They had three years like that, then a very bad year—Poppy was so gravely ill—and we lost her.

My first point about Přem is that I don't know anything about his mother. Karel would allow people to assume Přem is Poppy's son, but he almost certainly isn't. Of course, a downside of long-distance friendship is that it takes some time to become aware of a new factor in your friends' life. I do, however, find it extraordinary that, after a decade of quarterly lunches without any mention of a new partner, fling, or any development falling between those two posts, Karel introduced me to Přem, who looked to be all of ten years old.

I asked the little boy how old he was, and he smiled at me and said, "Guess!"

Karel had been ill for about a month prior; he characterised it as a stomach complaint and told me his doctor found nothing wrong, and I believed him at the time, but I don't anymore. I mean I believe Karel was laid low by what he called his stomach complaint, but I doubt he saw a doctor about it. He probably stayed at home all month, possibly feeling death draw near and shrinking away, and somewhere near the middle of all that Přem arrived. Dropped off by his mother, probably. I am volunteering this as a guess even though I don't believe it. I'm not sure what I do believe concerning Přemysl.

I paid Karel an impromptu visit one evening. I didn't tell him I was coming, I just took the train up to Newcastle and took a taxi to his house. That morning I had felt that something was the matter and that it might not be too late to fix it as long as I saw Karel that very day. Karel answered the door himself, looking better than I'd seen him in a while, and I felt as if I'd caught myself wishing bad things on him. I got a warm welcome and a cream tea from him, even though darkness was falling. We talked for hours. Přem was about seventeen by then. Karel was particularly pleased with how well he was doing at school, and was matter-of-fact about him continuing higher education close to home, so that he wouldn't be out at night. I asked him if he didn't think he was being too strict with Přem, and he began a circumspect answer, then his telephone rang upstairs. He excused himself; there was a call he'd been expecting all day. And almost as soon as he had gone, Přem was there. I don't mean he had come in, I mean he was there. There was a lamp beside the chair I was sitting in; he switched it on and said, "Yes, Ms. Rashid, he is too strict. Thank you for being on my side."

I may have simply gibbered for a moment; I just couldn't get my bearings. He told me that, because I was on his side, he wanted to give me a present. I think that's what he told me. Very strange, that night. When I think back to it, I think I must have . . . misunderstood somehow? "Misunderstood" doesn't seem to be the right word, but he was saying nonthreatening things at normal pitch, yet everything he said scared the hell out of me. There had to be a misunderstanding somewhere. Anyway, he said he wanted to give me a present. And I thought, whatever this present is, I certainly mustn't accept it. It was also beginning to be rather difficult to comprehend where exactly in the room he was. He switched on two more lamps and he seemed to be where they were and also by the bookcase and also, quite horribly, sitting at my feet with his elbows on my knees.

"A musician without an instrument," Přem said. "A woman who will never marry . . . hmmm . . . I've got just the thing for you all the same. Don't you want your present, Ms. Rashid?"

"No," I gasped. "Go to bed."

"But you'll like it. The present. I can bring you someone. Anyone you want. Just think of someone and I'll bring them."

"Bring someone? From where?"

He switched on another lamp and said, "Anywhere . . ."

Karel got off the phone and came back, thank God. He gave Přem a hearty clap on the shoulder: "Bedtime, right?"

"Bedtime," Přem agreed.

"I'll just say goodnight to Zeinab, and then I'll be
with you."

"Then you'll be with me."

I never visited Karel at home after dark again, even after
he assured me that Přem was now "much better at night."
There are a couple of other stories about Přem from when he
was ten or so; hearsay, so I'll be brief with these. The first is
that a pair of would-be kidnappers took Přem from the posh
primary school Karel was sending him to, but <u>returned him
in the middle of the night</u>. It's the middle-of-the-night bit
that made me think this actually could have happened; the
kidnappers saw what he was and just took him home. There
is this too: when Přem was asked for some description of the
kidnappers, he said that one was a white man and the other
was a white woman, that they were "not as old as my father,"
and both of them made him sad. Why . . . had they harmed
him somehow? "No," he said, "they were fine at first, but
then they started to look like this"—he drew two faces with
upside-down smiles—"and after that they just kept crying
and crying and crying . . . It was sad . . ."

The other bit of hearsay is to do with a violinist who
Karel mentored for a while; a somewhat pudgy young man
who was self-conscious about his weight. This violinist
volunteered to play for Přem at night but couldn't stay
awake. At around six in the morning, Karel found the young
man passed out in the second-floor bathtub with leeches
writhing all the way up to his chin. Alive, fortunately, and
later, the young man told a story (of sorts) about Přem

"bringing the leeches because he knew I wanted to be skinny. He said it was the easiest way." But Karel insisted this was "largely untrue," whatever that means, and the violinist stopped telling his Přemysl tale once Karel threatened to sue. We'll just have to shrug about that incident.

So far I have not been fair to Přem. As you will have seen for yourself, he was a great comfort to his father. His manner improved as he got older; at various points over the two decades I was in contact with him, I observed that he was getting kindlier, possibly sadder. He wasn't musical, but I know that he pursued the visual arts with quite a lot of energy. I've heard quite confused descriptions of a series of "white paintings" he produced, but never saw one. And then he burned them all.

Before that there was a row about being cut out of the will, of course, but I'm not so sure it was about the money and property. I was there with Karel in his study. Přem came in with a contract for Karel to sign, threw the contract down, and said: "Change the will."

Karel looked at him very coldly and asked what change Přem wished him to make.

"Leave it all to me. Your estate, or whatever it's called."

Karel snorted, but Přem said it again. "Leave it all to me. Unless . . . unless you think Ava's right?"

Ava, you will have to refer to whatever argument/s you may have had with Karel and/or Přem here . . . I was hoping Karel would say something that hinted at it, but he just continued glaring until Přem said: "So I have to die when you die, do I?"

Karel looked at me and told Přem to be quiet. Ordinarily that was enough; with Přem, Karel's word was law. But this time Přem went on. "It's always like this . . . Why is it always . . . you will leave me, Ava will leave me . . ."

Then Karel, mainly to stop Přem talking, I think, said that he was arranging things like this for Přem's sake. He spoke with his eyes on the contract Přem had brought in, turning pages and checking them before signing. He told Přem he mustn't look for a replacement, especially not in you, Ava.

"You have to try to be on your own."

I just stared down at the document the whole time; I had an idea that if I looked up, Přem would start talking about giving me a present again. You see, the worst of it was that I did want it—the present he said he had for me. He'd offered it seventeen years before and had shown me nothing but politeness after I'd turned him down, but I thought about it every day—a few times a day, actually—I should have accepted his gift—why was I so frightened of it? Now that I'm fairly certain he and I won't meet again, I can admit that I behaved somewhat awkwardly in Přem's company because I couldn't quite trust myself not to catch at his sleeve and ask for my present. An old biddy like me pawing at a strapping young man like him . . .

Anyway, Přem didn't speak to me that afternoon. Karel told him he had to try to be on his own, and he said something to the effect of "Karel, I will try to let go of her, but if I can't, it's not my fault." Then he picked up the contract Karel had signed and left.

Karel told me he didn't come home that night. The next bit of news I heard about Přem was that he'd moved out of Karel's house. They reconciled, or seemed to, about a year later, after Karel collapsed. Přem donated his kidney and was at home with Karel again for a while—they may have had "bad" nights again, because Karel couldn't play for Přem, and you'd stopped coming. This is inference, though, not anything I heard. You do have to wonder about his nights after he left Karel's house; I'm sure someone fitting Přem's description has left the good people of Dulwich with many a weird tale to ponder. Then, five months or so after Karel's transplant, there was Přem's art fire. And now . . . I suppose if there is anything more to know about Stojaspal, we have to wait for your birthday.

That said, I don't believe Přemysl will intervene in the matter of this inheritance, Ava. He stated an intention not to trouble you—at least that's what it sounded like to me. You've spent nights with him and been fine, so there isn't anything he can do to you now.

Write me back soonest.

With love,
Zeinab

15.

OTTO SHIN

Hi Ava,

I can't provide as much of a profile of your Přemysl as Allegra and Ms. Rashid have. I say "your Přemysl," because isn't he yours? Or didn't he want to be? It sounds to me like he was captivated by that treating-him-as-if-he-was-literally-nothing approach, and he went along with it as a way of ingratiating himself with you. Ah, true romance! (I have to get back at you a bit for saying that about me and X.) But seriously. You don't mention your Přem contacting you. I mean e-mails, phone calls, etc. Though actually if I were him, I'd probably stop short of sending "hello, I exist" e-mails too. Denying that you're a hipster makes you a hipster, and claiming that you exist means you don't.

I can make the claim for him, though. Přem exists.

Existed? I saw him. I'll follow Ms. De Souza's lead and tell you about the sighting, and then, just like her, I'll tell you about another meeting (well, another relationship, actually) that I think belongs here, though you may disagree.

The sighting first: five years ago, I turned thirty-three. The entire year was a trudge; I had a master's degree but couldn't teach English Lit to save my life. A student I was tutoring said to me: "Er . . . have you actually read the book, Mr. Montague?" The thing was, I had. Tens of times.

I couldn't find any other use for my qualifications, and I was coasting along on handyman jobs I kept botching so noticeably that I'd have to halve my fee in acknowledgment of the fact that a real handyman would have to be called in next. It was standard practice for me to only get the house address right on my third try. That was how I happened upon the fire; I was wandering around Dulwich, looking for my client's house, which I'd probably have found quite easily if I ever remembered to charge my phone with outings in mind. I approached a building hoping it was the house I was looking for. It wasn't. It was a dead-end house that closed off a street of much smarter-looking ones. There was a stretch of concrete between that house and the house closest to it, and from chimney to doorstep the whole building just looked back to front. Gave you a sense that you shouldn't come this way, that progress was behind you. But perhaps you already know this flat, Ava. Perhaps you visited, looking for your Prem somewhere in that mass of canvas ash.

I saw someone standing in a window on the first floor.

He was facing me but not watching the street; he had quite a
faraway look on his face. It was the man in that self-portrait
in the gallery car, Ava. I'm sure of what I saw, even if I'm not
sure that he was there. He was older and a bit more
bedraggled than he is in that painting, and he was wearing
one of those nautical-stripe T-shirts—blue and white—and
jeans. I saw and smelt smoke . . . chimney overflow or
something, I thought. Get this . . . I also heard the fire
alarm. But everything seemed so calm—there was no
commotion whatsoever from the houses just a few steps away
(maybe everyone was out?). Basically I told myself this was a
household mishap that was probably already under control.
Now very close to certain I had the wrong address again, I
went up to the front door and saw that this building was
divided into flats—I looked at the nameplates lined up
beside the doorbells, even though I knew the client I was on
my way to had the whole house to themselves. There were
three names, but I didn't see Přemysl's, in case you're
wondering. I did see the name J. Svoboda, but more about
that in a bit.

The front door was ajar, and someone called out to me
from inside: "Quickly, quickly!" I went in, and the hallway
was crammed with smoke . . . dozy little me finally woke up
to the fact that this was serious. There was an old man who
shouldn't have been in there breathing in that smoke; he was
coughing and confused, and for a split second he thought I
was a fireman, that the fire brigade was already there even
though he'd only just hung up from calling them. He told

me to help his son, or to stop his son, I still don't know
which. I just went back out into the fresh air, pushing the old
man in front of me; I called an ambulance for him, and
while I was on the line to the operator, I was looking up at
the window and Přemysl was still there. There were flames
behind him, quite close. I didn't see them, but I saw the
room changing colour. And Přemysl was looking at me.
Very, very scared, yet determined to stay where he was. The
old man—Karel—kept trying to hobble back into the
building; I was having to sort of bear hug him to keep in
place. And then the man in the window suddenly winked
out of sight, and just like that I was in the hallway, then at
the top of the stairs, then in through the open door of that
first-floor flat . . . I didn't decide; it was decided, and it was
done. There were four rooms, I think. The kitchen was just
after the entrance, smoky, but no flames yet. I ran a napkin
under the tap and put it over my face, then went into the
next room, and the next; rooms the fire wobbled around in
rings; I never thought it could do that, act like rampant jelly.
Or I saw it that way because my head was spinning and I
was asphyxiating. Anyway, I saw canvases burning, flapping
on their stands . . . I'm sure I'd have found it creepy if I
hadn't been struggling to breathe . . . I mean, they could've
doubled as a field of scarecrows come to life, those burning
canvases. But as we discussed earlier, Ava, there was no one
in the flat. In the bedroom, clothes were laid out on the bed.
A blue-and-white-striped T-shirt, jeans, socks where the feet
would be. I have described this over and over (to myself, to

concerned listeners, some of them professional listeners), but none of the details change. I kept saying to myself, Get out, get out, turn around, and I fell onto the bed. I think I said: "Oh gosh, sorry, sorry about that," because it seemed like I'd hurt someone . . . why did I think that . . . there might have been a sound? A sucking in of breath, like when you stub your toe but want to avoid histrionics? There was no one there, but before I passed out, it felt like someone stepped on me. Yes, stepped on me. Not to cause me pain—more a kind of acrobatic manoeuvre . . . to reach the ceiling . . . God, what am I saying to you, Ava. A heel pressed down on my chest, and I winked out of sight too.

It seems the firefighters burst in a couple of minutes after me—I got off very lightly in terms of physical issues. Everything else was a bit nightmarish for a while as the facts piled up . . . The entire building had been empty, not just the flat—the other two residents were out, and there were no witnesses regarding the arsonist. I really couldn't understand that at all, given what I had so unambiguously seen in broad daylight. Karel went on record with a statement that he'd been there to collect his son's post and hadn't seen what had happened. He was quite clearly grappling with something terminal too, so I think any initial suspicion that he'd committed arson soon evaporated. As for me, there was a sense that I'd stayed in the fire, or that I might as well have. My friend Spera all but moved in with me for the next few weeks and looked after all three of us Montague boys. Palliative care for Árpád XXIX in the last few days of her long life, nutritious feed and frolics for her youthful successor, plus a similarly rigorous watch kept on me. Thank God for Spera, even though on her second day of residence she decided the very look in my eyes had changed . . . I now had "the eyes of a sleeping phoenix." She kept snapping photos of me at inconvenient moments so she'd get what she called a candid expression. I put up with that and sought out cures for insomnia. Where were you and your theremin when I needed you, eh?

One of my mums' friends suggested hypnosis and recommended a therapist she was convinced had cured her own insomnia. The clinic was on Harley Street, so my mums had this reverence for it: "Can't go wrong with a Harley Street treatment . . ." They offered to pay for a few sessions with this hypnotherapist, so I booked an appointment and went along to the clinic with an open mind.

It was October 2014. The clocks had just gone backward, and I'd forgotten to inform my watch of this fact, my phone was dead . . . I'd missed my appointment by an hour . . . Oh, and the receptionist at the clinic was this naughty-looking, heavyset blonde with a deep voice that got me stiff and kept me there. He seemed about my age. A good sign, because, before him, age gaps exceeding seven years had been my personal recipe for heartache when partnering up with anybody. Something about the difference in life stages; that's what I was told whilst getting dumped, anyway. Another good sign: after a couple of months of being too shaken up by the fire for Eros to bother knocking at my door, every not-so-innocent word that receptionist said filled me with yearning. His name was Jan, but he said I could call him Honza. On my way out I went through the "I might have got the wrong idea, or maybe you're seeing someone, but here's my phone number anyway" speech. I didn't suggest friendship because I already knew that if I ever had another five minutes alone with him, I wasn't going to be able to pretend that I saw him as a potential friend. I mean, maybe later, but first things first. He took the scrap of paper from me, picked up the phone on the desk in front of him, and dialled my number. We both listened to my voicemail greeting, and he said: "You'll answer next time, right?"

I was never more conscientious about keeping my phone charged than I was during my seven months with Honza Svoboda. He didn't seem in any way aware of his drool-generating effect on pretty much any sexually available human being who crossed his path. He may have taken up the occasional offer—we never spent the night together, so I wouldn't know . . . He left the receptionist job and got a night job as a security guard. The most I usually got to do with him at night was walk him to work; we'd arrive at around ten p.m. at the latest, he'd change into uniform and send me home. This was usually after spending the day together, so I did sometimes wonder if and when Honza slept at all.

Honza was the one who instigated our monogamy discussion, and he was the first to say "I love you." He was OK with me not being ready to say it back, but he got

anxious about . . . I can't remember his exact terminology—
either being "enough" for me, or being "what I wanted."
He'd accuse me of looking elsewhere when I really wasn't. I
was his unemployed puppy who took everything he had to
give me. Psychoactive substances, days-of-the-week
underwear, mesmerism lessons. Yes, I'm a hypnotist because
of Honza. I'd told him I needed something to do . . . not just
for money, something that would put the fire and whatever
had made me run into it very firmly in the past. He said,
"Oh, if it's a pastime you want, I have just the thing . . ."
And he said it was easy to learn. Maybe it was for Honza. I
may not be accredited, and he didn't teach me to apply these
methods therapeutically, but unless I'm dealing with the
likes of my partner's aunt, the stuff I learnt from Honza
Svoboda works and has built me a substantial client base. I
didn't realise it while he was working on me (it probably
wouldn't have worked if I'd realised it) but this guy Honza
did as much as Spera did—maybe more—in terms of
putting me back on my feet, and in better stead than I'd
been before. Everything in living memory that had ever
worried me or caused me stealthy glee . . . I must have
discussed it all with Honza S. He was interested, he cared,
but he didn't respond with his own stuff. I didn't meet
Honza's friends, and I didn't get to introduce him to mine;
the plans kept falling through at the last minute. Árpád
didn't like him, but then Xavier Shin is the only boyfriend of
mine Árpád has ever shown enthusiasm for. I could tell from
the first night Xavier stayed over at my place that we were in

a new era of acceptance; in the morning there Xavier's shoes were, exactly where he'd left them by the door . . . unchewed and unshat in.

Honza didn't like Árpád either . . . I remember he never referred to Árpád by name; it was always "your friend the stoat," "that marten that aspires to mongoosehood," or "the vicious ferret." Honza also said he didn't need to meet my friends. He was happy with me as long as he was what I wanted. Or maybe it was "I'm happy with you as long as I'm enough for you." I got uncomfortable when he talked like that, so I remember the "oh no, not this again" feeling more than I do his actual words. Whatever the exact wording was, it was cock deflating. I started looking elsewhere. Well, not just looking. Honza began to bring it up in conversation, the inevitability that I would do that "now that I'd got what I wanted" from him. He'd tell me I really didn't need to do that, and that I could always ask him for more. Always. And when he talked like that, I went beyond uncomfortable . . . basically, the feeling Zeinab Rashid describes regarding being offered "a present" was familiar to me.

That's not why I'm mentioning Honza here, though. There's no one reason for a breakup, but quite early on in the relationship I developed a suspicion of him that never went away. It wasn't any of the irregularities I already mentioned . . . it was about the fire. He knew about it. It had happened in the building he used to live in. Honza was the J. Svoboda whose name I saw beside one of the doorbells. He told me there was a neighbourhood rumour that somebody had run into the fire. Why would anyone do that? he wondered. Whoever it was, he thought they should still be rewarded for what they'd tried to do.

You might think that would have made me inclined to tell Honza what it was the heroic fool had thought he was trying to do, but I resisted talking about it for a couple of months. Then it got too difficult not to tell him; after all, we'd talked about everything else.

Honza was dissatisfied with my account but didn't seem able to explain why. He believed me, and yet . . .

I told him all over again. I felt like I owed him at least that much. Honza got less and less satisfied with each repetition. Eventually it felt as if every conversation we had was a pretext for him to probe my memory of the fire. There were no slipups in his line of questioning . . . It was always about what I remembered and never about any memories of his . . . but I started to have strange thoughts. He was the arsonist, or he knew that there had been a man in the flat and he knew what had happened to the man, but he would never back up my account, he preferred me to live in doubt of my own stability . . . thoughts like that. And like I said, I wanted the fire left in the past. I met up with Honza and told him this face-to-face, in a coffee shop, so there were plenty of witnesses in case anything happened. I don't know what I thought would happen, but that step beyond discomfort when he'd insisted I could ask him for anything . . . I did have that in mind.

Honza didn't protest. I took that as his way of indicating

I wasn't "what he wanted" either. He thanked me for my honesty and left. I haven't heard from him since. And I did miss him, but, Ava, I was so happy to be able to work and think and talk without having to keep putting together that jigsaw puzzle that always had the same piece missing . . . plus that truly maddening suspicion that this person who kept telling me he loved me had the missing piece in his pocket. The name "Stojaspal" never came up between us. So whether this truly is Přemysl-related or not is up to you, I suppose. But I do think we should assume that he will come calling very soon, your Přemysl. I'm not clear on his motive(s?), and I certainly don't mean to scare or worry you, but I'm finding I can't overlook a possible connection between your Přemysl and my Honza. Or, at least, a link I'm sensing between Přemysl's disappearance and Honza's appearance. Please understand that these aren't things I would admit to anyone other than a fellow member of the Empty Room Club. We need to come up with a secret handshake.

Ava, you're here with five friends—Laura De Souza might say you don't have that kind of relationship with her, but she'd be lying—and two of those friends are mongooses. Přem (or whoever) doesn't stand a chance.

O.

16.

XAVIER SHIN

Dear Ava,

I never heard the name Přemysl Stojaspal until I came aboard this train. Having read the other contributions (apart from Otto's—I don't think we will consult each other's recollections), I'm of the opinion that "Přem" refers to a person who will not be seen again. The fire that almost every other contributor to this file mentions: let's just say that fire took him. But what I'm seeing is that there was something that "Přem" wanted. Wants? What if his longing outlasts him? What if this longing actually is him, and he was a living, breathing strategy for its fulfilment?

I'm thinking of the ways your Přem bridged supply and demand. There he was as the son who was a credit to his father, the kidney donor who couldn't have been a better match if he'd been tailor made. There he was as Allegra Yu's social gatekeeper. There he was sending Mr. Lin to Laura at the exact moment she felt she needed to meet someone . . . well, someone just like Mr. Lin. And so on. And when I look at matters in those light . . . as arrangements rather than relationships, the primary mover starts to look . . . familiar.

Four years ago, I met an acutely alluring man, and we got attached fast. There wasn't really enough mutual support for me to call it a relationship, but there wasn't anything illicit about it, so I can't call it an affair either. Anyway, we were together for four months. And a matter of days after we broke up, I met another man—a cutely alluring one this time, and embarked on a similarly brief yet heavy fling that lasted four months. I'd never had a year like that and hopefully never will again . . . when Christmas came around, I was practically a nervous wreck and had to give myself the gift of a period of solitude and chastity.

Ava, I believe the two men who left me in that state were the same person.

I'm not talking about a personality type. I'm stating that the second man was the first man revisiting me with a different approach. Until convinced otherwise, that is what happened.

I met the first man, Raúl Mateus, on the very first day of May 2015. This was at the wedding of two friends, one of whom I'd been in unrequited love with for years. Lovelier still: the friend who was not my unrequited love had asked me to help write his wedding speech . . . which had turned into me writing the whole thing. I watched that friend saying almost everything I wished I could say to the only man I would ever love, and the other guests laughed and went "awww" at the appropriate points. As for the fucker who should have been marrying me but was marrying a nice, nurturing boy who didn't even know what to say to him on the first day of the rest of their lives together, only planned to be there and keep on being there, steady pom pi pi . . . I couldn't even look at my stolen groom's face. I was drunker than I'd ever been, and I remember quite openly patting myself on the shoulder and saying, "It's OK, Xavier, you're doing well, and it will all work out in your next life." A bearded Mr. Short, Dark, and Handsome sat down next to me, handed me some mint tea, and kept his arm around the back of my chair while I sipped the tisane and started to sober up. He had very striking hazel eyes and had accentuated them with turquoise eyeliner and black mascara. When he looked at me birds, bees, butterflies, dragons, bats, every winged thing you can think of got together and threw a debutante ball in my thorax. I think I dribbled wine.

Raúl asked me if I'd written the wedding speech, and I neither confirmed nor denied, but asked why he was asking. He said that during certain passages my mouth had moved in unison with the speaker's. He said I was a good writer. I advised him not to say such things; I said if he kept it up, I might end up going home with him. His response: Did I say a good writer? I meant a very good writer. Back at his place a couple of hours later, he kept up the consoling assertions as I removed his three-piece suit. He was about ten years older than me and had this Buenos Aires accent that lent a tone of good-humoured irony to almost everything he said. But he wasn't bullshitting me with that opinion that I could write. He ghostwrote biographies himself and put me in touch with a commissioning editor at the publishing house he most frequently published with. Krakamiche Press . . . the one founded by Karel Stojaspal. I sent in a portfolio of writing samples and was finally able to detach myself from the payroll of Do Yeon-ssi's company, where I'd been drawing a salary for playing the half-secretarial, half-ambassadorial role of Decorative Nephew. I still work with that editor, and the classical-music-world names he pairs me with, even though Raúl doesn't anymore.

Raúl . . . my relationship with him burned out fast. We were both stunned, Raúl and I, when I blurted out that I loved him. I did, I think. At least, I remember why I thought so. When we spent time with the newlywed banes of my life, I hardly felt a pang and was mostly focused on Raúl. I took that as a sign of something profound.

Raúl told me he loved me too, and immediately proposed marriage . . . which was much too much. I told him I'd think about it and immersed myself in what I thought of as writerly life. Mostly holing myself up in my room working on my own (very bad) novel and hobnobbing with any literary types who happened to be around. I almost neglected the ghostwriting project I was actually under contract for, going through the motions with these lacklustre interviews with this ninety-something-year-old conductor whose life story I was supposed to be writing. We were quite fed up with each other, the conductor and I. She was frustrated at not being able to organise her thoughts well enough to write the book herself, and I had such an inflated view of my own abilities I felt they were wasted on trying to channel this conductor's voice. Eventually, with deadlines breathing down my neck and the editor expressing grave reservations regarding the pages I'd sent in, Raúl listened to the interview tapes with me and gave all these sensitive and patient suggestions . . . Every time I came to him he thought of questions I should be asking and allusions I should be picking up on . . . The conductor and I started talking, really talking with each other . . . The project started to flow . . . and in among the e-mails from my new debut author friends and the e-mails from the editor at Krakamiche, one came in from Raúl, saying he couldn't be with me anymore. He didn't say why. I'd got around to telling him I couldn't marry him, but I don't think that was it. I replied to Raúl's e-mail—several times, actually—apologizing for neglecting him, trying to explain myself, promising to improve, asking if we could meet in person to talk things over. He didn't write back. It was only when friends asked me what had happened with my wedding date that I realised they all thought I had invited him to Tom and Thahan's wedding. None of our friends knew Raúl, or had run into him before that day.

Maybe Raúl—"Raúl," I guess—had observed the desperation I was feeling over Thahan and thought to recycle it. Or upcycle it . . . alchemise it, even. He thought he could take the commonplace lead of that heartache I felt was killing me and turn it into . . .

Well. There I hit my limit. Whatever it was he had in mind, he very quickly realised I'm a miracle-free zone, and he cut his losses just as quickly.

If so, what was part two about? In September of that same year, 2015, I tried to turn my very bad novel into a goodish novel by subjecting it to a change of scene . . . I took it to my local library and worked on it there. That's where I met a librarian named Tolay Gul. He was also short and dark—I suppose that was my type at the time, guys you could mistake for Thahan from behind—but Tolay was scruffier, goofier, with a classic *jolie laide* grin and a big, booming laugh. I couldn't quite predict what would amuse him . . . sometimes I couldn't even predict where in the house he'd be when I woke up in the morning. I went from a couple of months of sleeping and waking all entangled with Raúl to waking up in an empty bed and opening cupboard doors cautiously in case Tolay was hiding in there.

The cupboard under the sink seemed to be his favourite—
open the door and out Tolay would roll with an ear-splitting
cry: **Ciiiiiiiiaoooooooo bambini!**

Raúl only seemed to read newspapers, English and South
American classic novels, and writing manuals . . . He was
the guy who'd set me up with a ghostwriting gig and
enjoyed quietly discussing practicalities in some corner of a
gastropub. Tolay, on the other hand, had read every avant-
garde text going, made spot-on book recommendations, and
was generally very circus circus and cocktail bars. His
favourite one had the severed limbs of Barbie dolls dangling
from the ceiling. We lounged about with drinks, showing
each other YouTube clips on our phones. And in the heavens
tiny fists slapped tiny knees and set thighs aquiver with
yearning, distress, mirth . . .

In spite of all the differences between Raúl and Tolay,
from tastes and interests to manner to body language to
expression of libido to way of speaking (could it have been
that they were **too** different?) I found myself addressing
Tolay as Raúl. I did that without wanting to or meaning to;
it just happened. Tolay neither corrected me, nor seemed
surprised or offended. A couple of times over at Tolay's
place, I started to explain who Raúl is, or who he had been
to me, anyway, but each time Tolay put some music on,
turned his speakers up extra loud, and started doing star
jumps.

I scrapped the novel I'd been working on while I met

him and started a new one—a narrative so far from my
everyday thoughts and interests that it felt inspired—indeed,
some nights I dreamt that Tolay dictated whole passages of
it. In the morning I found those nighttime scenes saved in
the same document as the other chapters. The tale concerned
a priest who tries to build a new type of instrument. A silent
harpsichord that assigns a shade of colour to each note on the
musical scale and displays those colours when a piece of
music is played. He experiments with rapidly whirling
rainbow ribbons and with stained glass. But the people will
not allow the instrument to exist. Not even as an idea. A
squad of philosophers attack it on a theoretical level, and
musicians and music lovers decry it as neither entertaining
nor gratifying to the senses. Over the course of his lifetime,
the priest has witnessed people defend and condone concepts
ten times as wicked and twenty times as dull as his ocular
harpsichord. He's stunned by the resistance to the thought
he's attempting to finish, and he enters a crisis of faith that
he's never really able to leave.

Zainab Rashid would instantly have recognized what I
wrote as the novella Karel Stojaspal wrote. Not the same
story in a different style, but the same story in the same style,
word for word, except that I came up with an ending. I can't
even feel proud of that; it's highly unlikely that the ending I
thought I'd come up with was actually my own. I didn't find
any of this out until I'd engaged a literary agent and that
literary agent had sold the book to a publisher . . . quite a
prominent one. (I get into a cold sweat when I think what

would have happened if I'd showed "my" harpsichord book to someone at Krakamiche Press.) Then Tolay Gul brought me a library copy of Karel's book and asked, laughingly, if I'd read it. I hadn't, but I'd plagiarised it all the same. To say I was humbled unto dust, to say that Tolay kept me on nervous-breakdown watch for about a month after that discovery, to say these things understate what was going on in my head. But eventually, after disentangling myself from contracts I'd signed for the harpsichord book, I was able to return to ghostwriting with absolutely no illusions about having any other path. And the second time I was the one who told Tolay I couldn't see him anymore. I sent him an e-mail very similar to the one Raúl had sent me. Slightly more apologetic, but equally unexplanatory. I could hardly write that I didn't even feel as if I deserved to drink water, let alone receive his affection. I would probably have sounded like I was accusing him of making it difficult to do anything other than receive—and that accusation was in fact lurking in me. But anyway. Tolay wrote back in just under sixty seconds, saying he understood. He had one last favour to ask.

He wanted me to attend the opening of a photography exhibition at a gallery in Shoreditch. The artist, Esperanza Kendeffy, was known for never selling any of her work as a single unit. She'd stated in interviews that isolating a single image for display disrupted unities between her works. From a buyer's perspective this basically meant paying for four or more images you didn't want because the artist insisted that they were in some way part and parcel of the one image you did want. Tolay asked me to steal a photo from the exhibition. He said it was only a tiny one, and described it in detail.

Don't worry if you can't manage it. I'm counting on you to make an effort, though.

If I did get the photo, I was to drop it off at his flat in Dulwich. More intriguingly—and perhaps this was my real reason for doing as he said—he told me that I might run into someone named Otto Montague, and that I should steer clear of that person. "Because that person is mine."

I asked Tolay what made him say that. I suppose my real question was something along the lines of: How come you've never said I'm yours? It's not that I wanted him to. But you're always curious when you're bypassed and someone else is chosen.

Tolay's answer: "He's truthful. Not with words, mind. His abuse of linguistic function is almost demonic. But when I watch what he does . . . I'm not happy with all I've seen, but yeah, it's truthful. You can't really take that away from him."

I soon learned that Tolay has a point there. You'd be stupid to take anything Otto Shin says at face value. My life partner lies. A lot. I confront him over it as often as I can. Does he do it for fun? He shakes his head. Is he playing some sort of game of informational one-upmanship?

Another shake of the head: "Look, it's an unfortunate thing, the lying. A lot of the time it would be easier to just state the facts. But on the bright side, Xavier . . . lying is probably the most human gesture anyone can make."

"What? Explain."

"Well . . . they all say one thing and do another. Every one of them."

"'They'?" I said. "'Them'?"

"Humans. Obviously."

"I see. So, just to be perfectly clear, in this context, you're deliberately going with 'they' and 'them' rather than 'we' and 'us'?"

"Do those word choices bother you?" Otto asked.

"Strangely, no."

"That's a relief."

I've also noticed that lying to Otto, just a bit, at random intervals, tends to bring out the best in him. But that's another story.

Back to Tolay Gul.

The photograph he wanted me to steal was a close-up of a bloodshot eye with a black pupil. A splintered black, like a fly holding still with its wings folded over its body. Everything that led up to the theft was difficult—this tall, slim blond guy kept following me around the gallery with a glass of wine in his hand and a coat over his arm. I checked him out a couple of times, and I probably would have said hi or something, but you've seen Otto, so you know he has that spiritual bard—like look about him, as if he's more suited to doublet and hose than jeans and a shirt, and he's about to start playing a lute and singing of a rose that no man may dare pluck. I thought he somehow knew that I'd come there to steal, and he was going to tell me not to live like that. I spent about twenty minutes standing near the photo Tolay wanted me to steal, mainly checking its attachment to the wall. And Otto approached me. He said, "For the past half hour I've been trying to think of a witty way to tell you I'm not the coat person, but I can't think of anything. I'm just . . . not the coat person."

I said: "What?"

"I'm not here to look after people's coats." He handed me the coat he'd been carrying around. It was my coat. Then I recalled handing him the coat as I entered the gallery. I'd been flustered by my secret mission, he was the nearest person to the door, and it's possible he seemed slightly more officious than the other partygoers.

Tolay had made a very simple request that I steer clear of this person, and the very first thing I did was draw his attention. Which made it even more necessary to prove that I wasn't altogether incompetent. I had to steal this photo. I asked Otto all about his day . . . Oh, Esperanza Kendeffy was a close friend of his? And he was part of a gang of joyful minions who'd been spending the day making sure her launch went well? I thought (all right—hoped) he hadn't noticed when I held my coat close to the wall and pulled the painting in underneath the wool—he seemed unconcerned, and even moved away after a few minutes to welcome some newcomers. ("Be not inhospitable to strangers, lest they be art critics in disguise . . .")

But as I was leaving with my loot, a gallery representative approached me and took my phone number so as to arrange delivery of the other four photos the following day.

I offered to put the photo back, but the representative laughed at me and pointed Otto out. He'd bought the batch for me. He says he got a substantial friendship discount, but . . . just in case he was lying, I've been buying him drinks ever since.

I took that photograph around to Tolay's in the morning, but his nearest neighbour told me he'd moved out. I e-mailed and called, but he never got back to me.

Every few months or so I send a message to the e-mail addresses I have for Raúl and for Tolay. I say hello. I tell them I still think of them, and that I'm sorry. About everything, really. I tried hard to keep things on a platonic basis with Otto, frequently reminded myself that he was out of bounds, had been placed there by a person I'd already disappointed more than enough. Otto helped for a while by projecting the impression that he's a good friend but a callous love interest or sexual partner. That showboat cynicism of his, the part of him that in some way disturbs me as much as a suppurating boil would—I can see how Tolay Gul would find that stimulating. Otto Shin is so much on the run—from conscience, from reflection, from admitting there's any future he hopes for or anything he dreams of becoming—that when I realised what I felt for him, I tried my best to send him packing. It's frustrating enough having ideals without somebody at your side routinely making a mockery of them.

But, just as Tolay Gul says he did before me, I found myself watching what Otto Shin actually does. Otto does kindnesses whilst attempting meanness. He empathises whilst affecting apathy. He's unable to extricate himself from hopeful undertakings. Deeds that probably won't change anybody's world for the better but just might. Otto Shin does all he can at the same time as firmly denying that he's doing anything, or that there's anything he can do.

About the eye in the photograph Tolay asked me to steal: it turned out to be Otto's. The photo is part of a series Spera Kendeffy captured while Otto was recovering from something that happened to him. He was in a house fire. Spera stayed with him and looked after him, but was also his sickbed paparazzo . . .

And now he's right here opposite me, scribbling, frowning, biting the end of his pen, and exuding kissability. I think it's time to stop writing about him. Time to interact!

Just a few more thoughts:

Ava, all may yet be well if we can find out what your Přem wants, or wanted. The subject of this file may (or may not) "bring leeches," inculcate wholescale plagiarism, and get up to all sorts of other things that make him hard to handle at night, but . . . I think we can see these outbursts as being linked to excessive enthusiasm. It's easy to overdo things in the sincere pursuit of tranquility.

Your entry continually links him to Karel, but try to recall what it was like when it was just the two of you, you and Přem . . . isn't he seeking something exactly like that?

X

17.

It was late afternoon by the time we'd finished our contributions to Ava's file on Přemysl Stojaspal. Xavier lay down on one side of the carriage, and I sat cross-legged on the other, both of us covering sentences with our wrists and casting sidelong glances at each other as we composed our thoughts, both of us looking out the window during extended periods of deliberation, working out what to tell and what to shut up about.

We passed pages from previous file entries back and forth. Allegra Yu's and Zeinab Rashid's were Xavier's most requested. He didn't believe their accounts, or didn't agree with their over-and-under interpretations of the information they had, or something. At some point during his fourth or fifth rereading, he pointed out A and Z really seemed not to like that their lonely widower had a descendant. Had one, or had wanted one. This cryptic son made his father's home peculiar and his behaviour even more so.

"I did pick up a bit of a tone there," I concurred. "An *ugh*, if you will. A suggestion that they would have preferred it if Karel's second attempt at family life hadn't taken this particular form. They didn't know what to make of the sudden son. And neither Přem nor Karel really gave them anything to go on."

"Right," Xavier said. "That tone we both picked up on isn't aimed at the fresh start but at the form these two"—he tapped Allegra's and Zeinab's entries—"saw it taking. Between them they make sure that form—Přem's form—is thoroughly hidden. What's left is a vaguely unsavoury lump held captive by their distaste for his supposed function. Bam, A and Z remove Přem's prefect badge and pin it to Ava's blazer. Their message to Ava: *You're* the appropriate protector and beneficiary of this man's worldly goods, and we hereby appoint you to this position. You're the one who fits into the tale of the artist who leaves nothing of artistic merit behind. You, Ava, saw that nothingness. Now take this money and this power. Vision is thicker than blood! With an extra dose of chagrin on Allegra's part for initially trying to follow Karel's formula."

I blinked. "Are you making this about men and women? Are you saying that childless females are enraged by males who only have male children because they can't stand witnessing the patriarchal power handoff right before their eyes? Or are you saying that females get upset with males who behave as if they're able to reproduce asexually? *Bow down before the womb?* Or what?"

Xavier drank some water, then made a face at me. "I said 'money and power' and you heard 'men and women.' Which words correlate with which in that fevered brain of yours? I wonder. No, the move I think Zeinab and Allegra are making in these accounts is the move titled *Art Is Made by Other People.* Or maybe even *Art Is Made* of *Other People.* We've got a teacher who, perhaps unconsciously, expresses and transmits a nonnegotiable criterion for art . . . that it speaks to posterity. It has to be born of isolation, then . . . at a distance from contemporary concerns. For this reason, and several others—yes, some of which are related to historical access, the teacher has neither the ability or the permission to make the kind of art she respects. Her impressionable students glean these views from her, and some of them are wounded in the same spot as Zeinab is. Allegra, for example. But others—for instance, Karel—feel no constraint at all. He had the resources to ascend to Olympus, but ultimately he couldn't hack it."

"Right under A's and Z's noses, he opts out of isolation and dialogue with posterity and opts into a bit of an inscrutable domestic situation, fair to middling film scores, and a prose piece he doesn't even finish . . ."

"Unforgivable," Xavier said. "And the figure of the son becomes a problem for them. A personal one."

I was listening, but glanced sideways while thinking about what he was saying. We were passing a billboard; had in fact been running alongside the advert it displayed for about thirty minutes, and every now and again we'd been hazarding guesses as to what was being advertised. Xavier allowed himself another sideways glance too. The advert (about four metres high and miles and miles and miles wide) was in its entirety, an inexorably repeated LOL in an italicised typeset. *LOLOLOLOLOLOLOLOLOL* . . . Oh, and punctuation appeared in the middle of each O, so that some represented smiling faces while others frowned, screamed, appeared to be verklempt or caught in the throes of anhedonia. We allowed the billboard to *LOL* at us for a while.

Xavier was the first to rouse himself.

"Otto. What was I saying?"

"Art Is Made of Other People . . ."

The train slowed, then stopped altogether. We'd pulled into a redbrick stabling yard. We watched as the merchants boarded, along with swathes of bazaar paraphernalia—baskets, banners, hampers trailing sequined scarves, rolled-up rugs. Allegra and a couple of members of the maintenance team were in conductor mode, checking passports and ticking off names as each new passenger walked up the train steps. After a few minutes, Laura joined them.

"Quick question, guys—" Ava said from the corridor. We both screamed. She'd braided her front hair into a lustrous little tail that wagged when she moved her head—I could picture Allegra tying the lilac ribbon at the end and issuing a decree that this was to be worn until nightfall. It was the same as with the black hearts drawn onto Allegra's cheekbones: even if these were little attentions each had paid to herself, they somehow seemed to have been undertaken on each other's behalf. Ava wagged her braid of front hair and held an envelope and was not in any way a fearsome apparition. We just hadn't been expecting her; she'd crept down the carriage so quietly, under cover of the bazaar commotion. She repeated herself once we'd calmed down. "Quick question. Do the names"—she glanced at two lines of black text scrawled across her left palm—"the names 'Honza Svoboda' and 'Raúl Mateus' ring a bell at all?"

In silence, we handed her our written accounts, along with the other four.

"Thanks," Ava said, sliding it all back into the folder and then stuffing the folder up under her jumper. "I was just in the postal-sorting carriage, you see . . ." She handed me the envelope and, beckoning Xavier, leaned on my shoulder as we inspected it. Ava's name was written across the front, and where a postage mark would have been, the words *Agency for Introducing a Sense of Proportion into Novel Writing* were stamped in blotchy red ink.

There were three sheets of paper inside the envelope. Letters; all three in more or less identical handwriting. I took them out one by one and read them aloud.

The first:

Dear Ava,

    You'd better not listen to them. They're a bad influence.

                            Yours sincerely,

                            Honza Svoboda

The second:

Dear Ava,

    You'd better stop talking to them. You're a bad influence.

                            Yours sincerely,

                            Raúl Mateus

The third was unsigned.

Nothing to add. Except—Ciiiiiiiiiaoooooooo bambini!

Something inside me curled and curdled, and Xavier murmured that we were probably going to go out of our minds before Ava did.

I tried to return the letters, but she wouldn't take them.

"Oh no . . . you keep them, please. I— Hang on." She raised a hand, frowning. "They're coming. Three . . . two . . . one . . ."

The connecting doors on either end of the carriage rolled open. Allegra came upon us from the direction of the library, and Laura from the direction of the pantry. Not smiling, exactly, but the mood they brought with them was lighthearted and low-key. A little too uniformly so.

"Ready to do some shopping?" Laura asked, shaking a pair of imaginary pom-poms.

"Chop chop, Ava," Allegra said. "All this is for you. Maybe you can find a nice present for Dr. Zachariah. Who will be with us tomorrow. Remember?" Laura and Allegra cast cheery glances at each other, then at us, then at their most important passenger, blithely ignoring the document-shaped bulge that lay across her bosom.

I got to my feet and checked for my wallet, unsure what was in the air or why this had been brought here to us in Clock Carriage, but ready to leave them to it. I was still holding the communication from the so-called Agency for Introducing a Sense of Proportion into Novel Writing, and after a few more moments' deliberation, I pushed the envelope and its contents out of the nearest window. "The, er, bazaar, does accept credit cards, right?" Xavier asked.

"Ah yes, Dr. Zachariah! What do you think I should buy for the doctor who's been such a rock all these years?" Ava turned to us with her arms spread, stage musical ingenue style.

Xavier began edging out of the compartment without a break in his musings regarding financing options for the bazaar. "I do have some hard currency—euro and pound sterling, and I always carry some Korean won, for sentimental reasons . . ."

Laura and Allegra had already moved aside for us, and I would have followed Xavier if only Ava hadn't been looking at us with . . . I'm not sure what, something like drunken amazement. As if she was trying really hard to get us into focus but the situation was really out of her hands and would therefore depend on us. *Stay there . . . I mean here . . . please just stay.*

"But cards are probably better because we might not be . . . in a place where pounds or euro or Korean won are in circulation," Xavier muttered. He stayed where he was, out in the corridor with Laura and Allegra, and I stayed where I was, with Ava, who swayed on her feet and said: "I think we're all just tired, aren't we? Do you think it'll be OK with the merchants if I shop lying down?"

Laura said: "It's your bazaar, Ms. Kapoor. If the merchants mind you lying down, they can get lost . . ."

Allegra tilted her head, observing, then moved past Xavier and reached for Ava. I wasn't sure of her intentions—probably tender? But Ava very clearly baulked at this advance, so I gave

Allegra a little tap with my elbow to keep her away. The chain reaction to this: Allegra walked backward until she bumped into the
furthest wall. Laura tutted with disgust and stepped forward to
administer a chop to my windpipe. Xavier, probably finding that a
bit of a disproportionate response to what I'd done, took firm hold
of Laura's wrist. I raised my own hand and gave my best impression of someone who had no qualms about slapping his attacker
silly. Xavier grabbed the hand I'd raised with his other hand.
Laura, Xavier, and I crossed arms and palms in a textbook Ba-
roque dance figure, only with more glowering. Ava tried and failed
to suppress a giggle. Laura peered at her, then stepped back with a
shrug. And then we all got out of Ava and Allegra's way.

Allegra cleared her throat. "Ava . . . we're so close," she offered
finally. "Just one more day. Could you—"

Ava's laughter got noisier, and the file on Přem slid back down
her jumper in bits and pieces. Paper poured down her legs and
covered her feet. Allegra looked down and read some of her own
words; her gaze travelled back up to Ava's face eventually, but it
was a very halting process.

"It might have been OK if you hadn't mentioned the doctor,"
Ava said. "God! It feels like you're obsessed with the optics of sanity." She knelt and gathered up sheets of paper. More paper rained
down. She shook the rest out of her jumper and started all over
again. She took deep breaths; the laughter died. "Anyway, you don't
need to worry about it anymore. I already passed the evaluation."

Allegra moved towards her again, and Ava's cheeks twitched,
but she maintained her composure, concentrating on reorganiz-
ing the file.

Very softly, Allegra said: "Ava? What are you doing, beb? Can you tell me what's happening?"

"Everything we wanted is happening," Ava said. "Everything we wanted. We're going to be rich. Dr. Zachariah boarded a few hours ago . . . we talked for ages . . . just ask her . . ."

Allegra's gaze swiveled to Laura, who lifted her clipboard, flipped some pages, and said: "No. The doctor will join us at ten a.m. tomorrow."

"What do you mean, ten a.m. tomorrow?" Ava giggled. "There she is."

"Where?"

"There. Right behind Laura."

We looked where Ava was pointing; we looked at Laura's shadow waxing and waning amid the motes of sunlight that flickered all along that otherwise vacant corridor. We looked at each other looking at Laura's shadow and satisfied ourselves that there was in fact a We, a We for whom the corridor was empty. A We that Ava Kapoor was, for the moment at least, not part of. And for the duration of that group mind illumination we kept silent, since none of us had the faintest idea how to proceed.

"Well?" Ava asked, still pointing.

Allegra swallowed hard. "That's a different doctor," she said, turning from us so that she was looking only at Ava.

"Different? Different how?"

Allegra shook her head, still refusing to look our way. We had a bit more silence, then Laura ventured: "To be more specific, Ms. Kapoor—it's a different Dr. Zachariah."

"Again . . . different how?"

"The main thing," Allegra intervened, "the main thing is that the pressure's off you now, beb. Our plan was too . . . heavy. I should have seen that. Can we—"

Ava gave a huge, horsey snort. "Ah . . . I can't keep this up. I was only fucking with you, sweethearts. Your faces, though! If you could all see yourselves right now . . ."

Her smile disappeared the split second Allegra swung for her. The first punch flew wide, but the second grazed her temple, and she scrambled to her feet and took the advice Allegra was doling out with additional blows: "Run, Ava! RUN. Get the fuck out of my sight right now. If I catch you I'm gonna tie you to the train tracks . . ."

Ava bolted for the library carriage, braid and ribbon whirling about her ears. We heard unrepentant whooping once she'd reached a safe distance. Also: "No, stop following me! Go away." Those words were for Xavier, but he paid no attention to them. We'd come back to it later, but I was reasonably sure of his take on Ava's little prank: some of it was just for laughs (her own, if nobody else's), and some of it was not. Now we had the beginnings of an inkling of what it's like to look on as everyone you know is all *Oh hiya, Prem*, and *What's the goss, Prem*, chatting away to a chair, a doorway, a poster on a wall.

Laura detained Allegra in Clock Carriage, pushing at her tear-splashed fists until they lowered and Allegra herself could be held and hugged and whispered to.

And me? I went shopping. Somebody had to.

18.

The bazaar was a faraway land I walked aeons to reach. Through the pantry car and the shower car and the postal-sorting carriage and the picture gallery car. The self-portrait of Přem ignored me, and the ground seemed to lick at my feet until I let that conveyor-belt sensation propel me into the dormitory car, with its many rows of bunk beds, each mattress a lily-white altar to innocence or incarceration. Notions came to me; mostly to do with Honza Svoboda. I won't put them into words, but some of those notions were so strong that they removed me from this sleeping carriage and placed me right in Honza's arms. My blood bobbed and weaved within me until I had to sit down on one of the beds and close my hand around the thin jerking of the pulse in my neck. I tried to conceive of offerings I could make in order to finish this thing with Honza. I'm not claiming that I deserve to be able to go through life with stanzas from the poem that is Xavier Shin on my lips and in my heart. It's not about merit . . . this miracle can happen because Xavier likes having me around as well.

For all I know, this is his favourite hobby: colliding with somebody who had made their mind up, taking that person by the
hand and casting such an abundance of moonlight that the one
he's with begins to perceive evidence they'd overlooked when preparing their estimation of this dingy world. Evidence that makes
the verdict unjust.

"Honza," I said, in case he could hear me. If he could, he
might write me a mocking letter about it. "Leave us alone."

All of the offerings that occurred to me involved the spilling of
vital fluids. If there'd been a suitable object at hand, I would have
made a cut. An interior voice—quite a nasty one, I think—asked
about the depth of the intended cut and insisted that if I chose to
make a blood offering I should do it properly and be sure to slit
my throat from ear to ear. The harangue ended when I admitted
that even if I had a knife in a hand, I wouldn't have made a cut.
But there was a backup offering, a sort of negotiation with the
memory of our bodies together, mine and Honza's. I closed my
eyes and saw our combinations: I knelt before him, knelt above
him, straddled him, stretched forward for him, swung from the
bunk bed ladders. I was a one-person ritual masturbation tournament, and those rows of bunk beds had probably never seen anything quite like the rampage I went on among them. Or so I like
to think. I painted the bed linen, white on white, just like Přem's
canvas, and I hid shivering under blankets every time I thought I
heard one of the others heading in the direction of the dormitory
car. I couldn't let anybody catch me doing this. Even if Honza
himself had arrived the offering would've been ruined.

In the fullness of time the ritual concluded, leaving yours truly physically spent. I took a nap on a top bunk, and some people may have passed through the carriage then—or there was hubbub from the picture gallery next door. I heard people, but nobody tried to wake me.

When I did wake, of my own accord, it was with the thought that vital fluids wouldn't be the appeasers in this situation. The one offering Honza was after was an answer to his questions about what I tried to do for that old man's son. If I told him that, he'd finally accept our breakup and get lost.

Why had I rushed into the flames for this person I saw, or thought I saw? (What was that? Was it love? Agape, philia, or a passion felt at first [or final] sight?)

But Honza's question can't actually be answered. It's a trick question, and he knows it. Answering it invalidates everything. What do I mean by "everything"? Everything everything.

I climbed down from the top bunk, gathered various far-flung pieces of clothing, got dressed, and crossed over into the bazaar carriage, too fuzzy-brained to register shame. I was sure the maintenance team were going to talk about the stains I'd left in that dormitory. I'd be lucky if they didn't report it to Ava. I tried to recall the name of the male maintenance team member I'd heard Allegra talking to via walkie-talkie. Edwin? Oliver? I wasn't sure what he looked like (there were eight or nine possible candidates), but I was going to pin this on him anyway. "I'm afraid I don't know anything about this, but why don't you have a chat with Edwin or Oliver?" I'd say. "Maybe he saw something."

The bazaar didn't accept credit cards. I knew it before I was told. Some of the stallholders seemed to have resigned themselves to shopper no-show and were sitting on stools gossiping over cups of tea and shots of vodka. Those stallholders didn't look my way, and neither did the ones who were painting each other's nails and giving each other shoulder massages. Right beside the entrance, a black girl in her midteens was tending to a slate water wheel that stood in a stone bowl about the size of a Hula-Hoop. This girl, who'd been painted gold from head to toe, was the official beginning of the bazaar. She sent a very clear message to anyone who walked in wondering if their cards would be accepted here, this girl painted gold and dressed in a gold leotard and gold socks to match her Mary Janes. She'd set a cap of gold wire and pearls atop her cornrows, and the slate wheel sang to itself as she let water fall from the golden jug she held. She varied the force of each pour. A caress here; an injury there. When the spokes of the wheel idled to a sulky *click click click*, the girl poured steadily from two jugs at once and sang a round robin with the wheel, putting words to its glad tintinnabulations.

"Hello," the girl said, when she noticed me.

"Hello. I'm Otto."

We shook hands. The girl said her name was Paz. And she asked me if I wanted to buy the water wheel. "You're one of the non-honeymoon honeymooners, no? Don't you think it would make a romantic gift? It is very simple to operate and to sing with, as you have seen."

The presentation of the wheel told you all you needed to know. It was the kind of item that could only be purchased with doubloons pulled from a treasure chest you'd wrenched out of the keeping of a deep-sea skeleton.

"Er . . . I'm actually not carrying any cash, but maybe Xavier—"

"Don't you want to know how much it costs?"

"Go on, then. Tell me."

She whispered the price in my ear, paused, then whispered an adjusted price that factored in a seven-year installment payment plan. I looked at the water wheel again.

"I don't think anybody's going to take this wheel off your hands, Paz," I said.

"What a pity," she said happily. She dipped her two gold jugs into the water at the base of the wheel and waved me onward, adding over her shoulder: "We accept cheques."

Moving from stall to stall I sipped tea, watched a snail race, became referee of the snail race and arbitrated a doping scandal, sipped vodka, sipped tea laced with vodka, kept forgetting I don't have a chequebook. I haggled half-heartedly over a pinhole camera I thought Spera might like, and almost bought moonstone and labradorite scrying balls for my mothers. Not because my mothers are especially into scrying or meditation, but because Dean, the holder of that stall, had gone to great lengths to source some of the pieces he'd laid out on display. Allegra had written to him months ago asking him to put together a scrying edit for Ava. Now that Ava was seemingly no longer bothered about looking into the future, I still thought Dean should have something to show for the time and care he'd put into gathering this row of globes. Each one was the flawed vessel of a perfect storm. But Dean said not to worry about it. He'd been fending off buyers for months. He wanted to give me a tip, though, for when I was doing my Christmas shopping and what not: "Bringing a scrying ball into a home that ain't in touch with its own clairvoyance? That's just asking for trouble. Just think about it, mate. You know it makes sense."

"Non-honeymoon honeymooner!" Paz the Golden pounced before I could move on to the next stall. "You still haven't bought anything," she said, and showed me a handful of cut emeralds. "What about these?"

Emeralds . . .

She swirled the stones, and their colour crackled. I'd pictured stones like those the first time I'd heard a friend call an aubergine "garden egg." Green shells that hatch long vines.

I recoiled without quite knowing why and asked sharply, too sharply, where she'd got them. Looking crestfallen, Paz lifted a dazzling arm and pointed to a stall near the end of the carriage. The stallholder was only dimly visible through a wall of cages. They were wearing a lot of costume jewellery.

"What's in those cages, Paz? I can't see from here."

"Taxidermized animals," Paz said. "They're his speciality."

"This guy sells emeralds and taxidermized animals?"

"That's right. There's this gigantic parrot that looks like it's having a nightmare forever and ever." She reflected a moment. "I really don't like the parrot. But maybe you would? Since you don't like the emeralds, and I do?"

"It's worth a try," I said. "Introduce us, please, Paz?"

"That's the spirit! Be friendly to me, honeymooner. He'll give you a good discount if he thinks we're friends."

I should have been looking ahead as Paz the Golden took my hand and led me past the other stalls, but we kept passing people and situations I couldn't let go without one more glance. I had to turn and berate the stallholder who'd popped an unwanted Pallas Athena style helmet on my head. I had to turn and thank the person who removed the helmet and daubed my wrist with jasmine oil. I had to turn and ask for more information on the crunchy, spicy, and/or worryingly mushy tidbits that had just been popped into my mouth by one stallholder after another. The onboard train bazaar was in overdrive for its lone shopper. And then, just like that, we were at the counter of the emerald and taxidermized animal stall, Paz was pouring her handful of emeralds into the velvet pouch that had been left beside the sign, and I was standing nose to nose with a stuffed mongoose in a cage. Two mongooses, actually. They'd been sawn in half and sewn together.

This cannot, this cannot, cannot be.

Nose to nose, eye to eye. Chela I may not know so well; the feel of her paw in my hand, that's already faded. But I know Árpád Montague XXX, from the downy tips of his ears to his graceful flanks to his balletic toes. It was him. It was them.

I didn't speak for what felt like a few minutes but was probably only seconds.

Once I was absolutely sure I wasn't going to throw up, I said: "Why are they in these cages."

Paz jabbed a finger at the 15 MINUTES BREAK sign on the counter and said of the man who'd left it there: "According to him, they move sometimes. Bite, even!"

I put my fingers through the bars of the cage, to try to stroke the fur. Paz went quiet, but her sigh showed she now understood she probably wouldn't be making a sale here.

My fingers and thumb brushed, tapped, then flicked the mongoose's back. Papier-mâché and synthetic fibres, united so tenuously that one touch damaged them. Hence the cages. Ha! I only had a moment to take that in before I heard Xavier's voice in the crowd behind me, but looking back I feel like that was the moment I broke faith with Árpád, with all the Árpáds who lived and died alongside the Montagues. When I looked at a not particularly well-made figurine and mistook it for Árpád and Chela. There's just no excuse for it.

I moved in Xavier's direction, listening to what he was telling the stallholders. He was clearing the premises, directing everybody in the carriage out onto the platform, answering questions and complaints alike with: "Sorry . . . I'm so sorry about this . . . We need everybody off the train . . . yes, maintenance team, too . . . Sorry . . ."

He told the stallholders Ms. Kapoor had asked him to assure them they'd get all their items back in good condition. She'd purchase any damaged items. Yes, any. She guaranteed it.

I found Xavier at the heart of the milling crowd and seized his hand.

"Awww, three cheers for the non-honeymoon honeymooners," roared Dean from the scrying crystal stall.

The crowd obliged. Hurrah for love! And then the two of us ("Quick," Xavier mumbled, "Quick, quick, quick—") helped Paz relocate her water wheel to the stabling yard platform. At every stage she explained that really she was helping out, taking the wheel with her. There was no way our Ms. Kapoor could afford it.

Paz the Golden was the last stallholder to disembark. She

waved at us with both hands, and I saw that the palm of her right hand, the one that had held the emeralds, was now She-Hulk green. She said something I didn't catch, and couldn't stay for, as Xavier had slammed the train door and was running ahead of me through the dormitory car, shouting that Yuri was here. Árpád and Chela had caught him and brought him to us.

By the time we reached the sauna car, Xavier was repeating himself on loop: *Yuri's here, Árpád and Chela caught him* . . . and I was trying to ask: "Has Ava . . . Can Ava . . . ?" but it was as if this news had broken both our vocabularies.

The third steam cubicle was occupied; we both saw that quite distinctly as we passed it. One after the other, we said, "Ava?"

She sighed but made no other reply, just let us go by without a word.

19.

I'd love to be able to describe Yuri for you, but I really never found out much. I never even heard his speaking voice clearly. Having compared notes with Xavier, this is what we've got for you. Height: Around five eleven. Hair: brown. Physique: the melted oblong of an out-of-shape wrestler. And there we hit the limit of our recollection. This was partly down to a toned-down version of the same processing problem I'd had with him before, when he'd come onboard in pajamas. But there's also the fact that this time he was wearing a full-face diving mask. Every facial feature was pressed down under clear plastic and tempered glass, so that whole area looked like a template more than anything else. I should at least be able to describe his eyes, since I looked into them for quite a while. It was a highly enjoyable stare. Nuanced as fuck. Like the very best of arthouse cinema. However. What colour are Yuri's eyes? Not a clue.

We had our stare, and then I asked him if he had any questions for me.

"None whatsoever," he said. "You?"

I did. I looked around at Xavier, Laura, and Allegra, and I asked Yuri if he was going to kill us. This seemed to shock him. "What?" he said. "You've changed, Otto. You didn't used to over-dramatise situations this way."

Was my question really that startling? The four of us were sitting with our backs to the train wall, our legs bound at the ankles, and our arms tied at the wrists. That was Yuri's doing. Laura had a black eye, and Allegra's nose was bloodied. Also Yuri's doing.

Silly us for getting all worked up about these things. Yuri explained that he actually liked us. Some more than others, but he was about to put all four of us in danger anyway.

"Exciting times for this pair of nineteen eighties babies . . . oh hurray, hurray for your generation," he said, kicking Xavier, then me, then Xavier, then me. "Rationing intimacy like it's wartime butter. Tolay was single, you were single, you fancied each other, shared interests, Honza needed a lot of help believing in himself, you needed a lot of help believing in yourself—"

(Kick, kick)

"You two could have built Honza and Tolay up, you could've really had something beautiful with them, spread the nurture around a bit—"

(Kick, kick.)

"But noooooooo, you still felt like you could do better, didn't you, Otto and Xavier?"

(Kick, kick, plus a nimble zigzag between our legs as we rolled around, trying to trip him up.)

"And have you? *Have* you done better? With each other?"

(Kick. Seeing that Yuri had completely succumbed to his own mask-muffled diatribe and really wasn't going to give it a rest with the kicking, the fight went out of me. I had another go at fainting.)

"Does this meet your high standards?"

(Kick, kick. I still hadn't managed to faint. So I very clearly remember Xavier shouting that he was going to tell on Yuri to Do Yeon-ssi.*)

Hang on.

I should go back a bit, to when Xavier and I ran into the carriage near the front of the train. The one Ava shared with Allegra and Laura.

Slowing it down for you, my observations in order: Allegra and Laura had been drinking tea at the kitchen table; they stood up when we came in. Pages from our collective file on Přemysl Stojaspal littered the tabletop, along with a number of highlighter pens. This shouldn't have been allowed to happen on Xavier's watch, and I said as much. (*"Aigoo,"* Xavier said, kissing two fingers and touching them to my lips.) Next I glanced at Ava's sleeping compartment, even though I knew she wasn't there. Her theremin was all set up for playing. Chela opened and closed her eyes at us in rapid sequence; a greeting in affectionate amber-lit Morse code. And Árpád, never one for long reunion speeches, simply whisked his tail in our direction. Laura predicted they

---

* Xavier disputes this recollection. However, since the kicking stopped immediately after this disputed statement was made, I'm leaving it in until Xavier is able to supply an alternative yet similarly influential factor.

would give this world some "badass descendants," and Allegra agreed: "Beginning with Chela Kapoor II."

Huh. Well, the age of the Árpáds can't last forever.

I've left the most incongruous feature of this train carriage scenario for last: a figure I might not have automatically viewed as Árpád and Chela's quarry if not for their watchful stirring whenever he stirred. He was standing in the lounge area wearing a diving mask, yellow swim fins and a peacock green wetsuit. His oxygen cylinder was still strapped to his back, and in his left hand he held a white balloon on a string. "A peace offering," he said.

So, this was Yuri. I reserved comment until I'd looked him over. He told me to take my time, and I did, slowly reconciling myself to the presence of this being who stoically dripped water all over the rug as his white balloon bobbed from side to side. The others had accepted the fact of him too; I could see it in their eyes.

Wondering aloud what was taking Ava so long, Laura drummed her fingers against the tabletop, drained her tea, then turned to Yuri.

"Well, Yuri. The mongooses have brought you to us because—"

We were all listening for the conclusion of this sentence with intense interest. We didn't know the reason. Did Laura? What? How? But Yuri cut her off with his own declaration.

"I brought each one of you to this train, of course. And long after you realised you weren't exactly brought together for a fucking Girl Scout badge ceremony, you've stayed on. Because I've kept you here. Well, really, you've kept each other here, with your eagerness to form a clique of people something out of the ordinary is happening to. Mundane jobs and Instagrammable honeymoons? Oh no, not for us. *We're* the passengers of *The Lucky Day* . . . ahem . . . hello . . . excuse me?"

The four of us were muttering to each other, exchanging notes as to whether this Yuri sounded anything like the way we remembered him sounding . . . "him" being Přemysl, Honza, Raúl, Tolay. He was telling us he'd brought each one of us here, but I, for one, didn't feel at all acquainted with this person. This was very much a meeting for the very first time. The others seemed to agree. The consensus was topped with a sprinkle of relief. Honza hadn't come after me after all . . . now nobody else would know how bad I'd been at being with him. I got the feeling Allegra shared my relief (with her own variation on the theme), and Xavier didn't. As for Laura, she gave confusion the middle finger and recommitted to some semblance of order.

"Pardon me, er—Mister," Laura said. "What did you say your surname was?"

Yuri unzipped his wetsuit and ran his hand around his chest for a few seconds. It looked as if he was gloating over his sheer, hairy manliness, but then he winced. "Found it . . ." He pulled his necklace over his head—it was a needle with thread looped through its eye.

He took a deep breath, then popped the white balloon with the needle.

The air . . . atomised . . .

. . . and then every particle of it twitched.

This was not the kind of situation consciousness is in any way equipped to cope with, so my "I" fled over the hills and far away, yodeling as it went.

It returned once it realised it had nowhere else to go. Why else would you return to a situation that's only very marginally less stressful? Ridges of train carriage wall digging into your back, hands crossed over your chest like the dearly departed who is about to be lowered into the ground, Árpád and Chela snarling away in his'n'hers cages, Yuri crouching down in front of you for just long enough to unzip your jeans and leer as he points out that you're not wearing your Czech day-of-the-week underwear. "Ha! I knew it . . . I knew Svoboda was fooling himself that you liked those boxers."

Xavier was to my left, with Laura on the other side of him, and Allegra on the other side of Laura. Yuri paced before us as he told his cautionary tale. We could not envisage, he told us, the things that had happened to Přemysl Stojaspal, to the truth of that person's life, from the moment Ava Kapoor had arrived at his father's house and unseen him.

"All right, so Přem hadn't yet learned stability. All right, so Přem was in essence a hitchhiker of sorts . . . actually, no, you know what, Přem was paying his way. We can compare him to an Uber rider . . . a slightly uncomfortable first-time Uber rider who was still getting used to the system. And then Ava Kapoor unsees him and his payment gets declined and his account deactivated. Of course he's going to try again with a new account. Of course he's going to look into other transport options! Of course he's going to try everything he can until his dream comes true! What dream? The dream of a pedestrian existence, my friends. Stupendously pedestrian. Oh, and to appear in photographs. You can paint as many portraits as you please, but it's photos that verify you people's meetings. It's photos that make your bonds irrefutable. Oh, are you laughing, Otto? Do it one more time . . . I dare you."

Dare declined.

Each of us stuttered questions, but Yuri waved them away. He hadn't come to engage with technical theories of Přem's unseeing, nor the question of whether Ava had done it intentionally. He was here to force us to consider the effect of the unseeing. According to Yuri, Přemysl was far from the only person to have gone through this process, and that Ava was far from the only unseer.

"We're trying to support each other," Yuri said. "Trying to get back into the game. Together. So don't ask me for my fucking surname. I'm here for Přem and Raúl and Tolay and the stories of their unseeing, which you will not be told now or ever. Because with people like you it goes in one ear and out the other until it actually happens to you. Then you'll be googling for support groups and everything else."

You'd think that afternoon we shared with Yuri was much more stressful in and of itself than the memory of it could ever be, but in fact I've had to abandon this account quite a few times already. I've had to drop my pen and hide from the page, only creeping back to it once Xavier sounds the all clear.

But at the time . . .

When Yuri had reached his "no more talking" phase, stopping

in front of Laura and Allegra and fondling their scalps before clapping their skulls together. Neither woman screamed, but Allegra murmured something. I thought I heard "Ava." "What did you say? What did you say, treacherous little bitch who saw what was happening to Přem and didn't stick up for him even once?"

Allegra closed her eyes but didn't shrink from Yuri. She said: "I don't know what you mean."

Her phrasing . . . she wasn't telling him *I don't understand what you're saying.* The sense of it came through as *I am unable to determine the meaning of you.*

I can be this precise because I was looking on with a stomach flutter. A very low-level flutter, and that was it. I've mentioned my assumption that nothing is ever OK. Even on good days I renew my nothing-is-ever-OK subscription so the next day is covered. It's a form of mithridatism. Once the poison is administered you still feel fear, but not as much as you might have, maybe. The other possibility is that the tension got so raucous that it blocked itself. Fear either gives you diarrhea or it really, horribly constipates you . . . something like that.

I remember hearing Xavier telling Yuri he was fucking trash, unrecyclable trash, and I remember Xavier toppling onto Laura's lap in a failed attempt to throw himself in front of her, and Yuri bashed Laura's and Allegra's heads together a couple more times, seemingly to show that none of Xavier's feedback bothered him.

I remember speaking, in a low and soothing voice. Not self-soothing; I was speaking to Xavier. I was saying, "Xavier, there's this train that used to belong to some tea smugglers, and it's called *The Lucky Day*. From the station platform it looks an outsized champagne sabre; a brass-and-silver curio with a snobbish tilt to its nose. Inside . . . well, there's no one onboard. There never is. At each station the passengers always arrive too late for *The Lucky Day*. Now the train's departing again . . . it's already waited as long as it could, and nobody came."

Xavier's head had lolled onto my shoulder, and when I paused, he scraped his cheek against my collarbone and told me he didn't understand a word, that at some point we were going to have to talk about my episodes of Czech speaking, but that for now I should go on. I might have, but if I did, I didn't hear it. What I heard instead, a little while later, was my own name. Maybe the others had been saying and whispering it on and off for ages. Laura had put her teeth to work gnawing away at the knots that bound her wrists, so Allegra's voice was the least garbled.

"Otto . . . Otto. What the fuck! Aren't you a mesmerist! How did you let things get this far? Mesmerise him or something!"

"OK, no prob," I said.

I looked up, down, to the left, and to the right, and didn't see Yuri anywhere. For about two seconds, angels sang: *Yuri is vanish'd, Yuri is vanquish'd, thou hast unseen Yuri*, but then the man in the diving suit stepped back into the carriage with us. He was carrying a pirate sword, which revealed he'd been to the bazaar carriage. And he was fuming again. This time over Ava. He'd gone to the sauna car to check what was taking her so long and found that she'd moved on to the greenhouse car. So he'd hung around while she did a leisurely spot of greenhouse gardening, thinking she'd start worrying about her friends ("Wasn't that a scream I heard?" etc.), but it looked like Ava was thoroughly fed up with us. Without even glancing behind her she'd proceeded into the library carriage, where she'd curled up with multiple books. At this rate she wasn't going to come back this way for hours. But she had to. He didn't have a single thing left to say to us . . .

Yuri's diving mask was getting all steamed up. He slashed at the air with the blade of his pirate sword a couple of times.

Xavier blurted out a suggestion. "Send Árpád. Or Chela. Both. She may be wily enough to slip through the clutches of one mongoose, but she could never evade two."

Yuri looked at the ceiling for a second, then shrugged and unlatched the cages. Árpád and our daughter-in-law were unsteady on their feet for a few heartbeats, but once they regained balance, it was all Yuri could do to lure them into the next carriage without a fatality (his own). Only the pirate sword saved him.

He stepped back into our carriage once more, the angel choir fell silent once more, and then, before he could pick up where he'd left off with the sword swishing, I said, "Why not let me mesmerise you while we wait?"

"Mesmerise me, then, Otto," he said, and came over to deliver his stare. That nuanced stare that I've already told you about. The one that ended up mesmerising me. Listen, I think Honza was there in that gaze. There was a look he gave me often. A *God, we're so pathetic and I fucking cherish that* look. As if we'd teamed up for a three-legged race and had the peculiar dignity of crossing the finish line behind everyone else on the planet. Yeah, Honza was there. All too briefly; I don't think "my" Honza Svoboda would have given us the kicking Yuri Don't-Ask-About-My-Surname did.

Very soon after the kicking, Ava Kapoor crossed over from the sauna car with a mongoose on each shoulder.

20.

She stayed near the door for a few seconds, holding on to the button that held it open, and all four of us wriggled towards her, ducking blows from Yuri's pirate sword, which he was using like a cricket bat, swinging away at our heads.

"Ava, look . . ."

"Ava, you've got to—"

"Ms. Kapoor, you must see this, you must see what he's doing—"

"*Ava*—"

What must that have been like for her? We probably looked and sounded like a pandemonium of parrots that had been cooped up for weeks. Our squawking contortions. Our bloodied drool.

At that point, even though she'd been so cold, bathing and reading books while Yuri bullied us, we still believed Ava was going to vanquish Yuri or take up our cause in some other way. So we wriggled on, preparing to lie at her feet until she relented. But Árpád and Chela held us at bay, and Ava made straight for her sleeping compartment, steering the widest possible berth around each one of us. Yuri lowered his sword and gave her a thumbs-up as she went. "Loving this new no-nonsense attitude," he said to her. "Ava Kapoor, Ava Kapoor, the most rational girl in town!"

She hesitated before stepping into her cabin. "You're not getting up?" she said to us. Xavier and I got death glares, but she was less sure she understood what was going on with Laura and Allegra. Her gaze trembled over and around their wounds.

Xavier raised his bound hands. "OK, but if you could just—"

"No, you've put on your little show, and you spoilt the bazaar, and you've made it clear what I'll have to tell Dr. Zachariah tomorrow—"

("What are you going to say to Dr. Zachariah?!" we all said, more or less at once. Yuri included.)

". . . so get up, everyone, and let's get going again. And as for you two Shins! You're a disgrace. I've seen the state of dormitory carriage, and I expect those beds to be stripped by the time we drop you off. I mean it. You've had a whole two carriages for your private use and it wasn't enough . . ."

"Oh, those two always want more, Ava," Yuri said, nodding sagely. He walked over to the lounge area and took a seat. Árpád and Chela kept monitoring him, sizing up their chances of jumping him, but he never let go of the pirate sword.

Xavier looked at me and mouthed, *What?* I mirrored him, and Allegra rested her bruised forehead on her steepled hands while Laura made one more formal plea for Ava to look over her shoulder—just over there, at the chair that was now facing Ava's sleeping compartment. Laura began to describe the details for

Ava. The wetsuit, the full-faced diving mask, the pirate sword. She trailed off as she listened to her own description. But she'd briefly sparked Ava's interest: "You're seeing all that over there?"

She flicked a brief glance at Yuri. I mean, directly at Yuri. We all saw it. Disconcerted, he waved at her. Had eye contact been made, though? That was less certain. Ava turned back to us. "Come on, guys. I'm sorry if I worried you earlier. And this—it's almost flattering that you'd go to this much effort . . . but . . . it'd be lovely if you'd just get up and we could put this behind us."

Allegra, head still pressed to her fingertips, said faintly: "Ava. Beb. I don't know how to describe this situation to you in a way that isn't going to piss you off, but if you untie just one set of hands . . . doesn't matter which . . . we'll all be free very soon, and—and then we'll be on our way to the doctor . . . within the . . ."

Ava was already at her side, an arm around her as she rummaged through floor-level drawers for a knife suited to rope cutting. We could see a number of questions occurring to her as she sawed away, but for the time being she contented herself with one.

"Allegra, who did this?"

Yuri leapt to his feet, excited. "Přem! Tell her it was Přem. Say: *He sends his regards*, and then burst into tears. Go on. I'll give you a tenner."

Ava touched her forehead to Allegra's. "Allegra."

"Allegra," Yuri said. "Pssst, Allegra. Twenty pounds cash in hand if you tell her she's the one who did this."

Then he asked me if I'd lend him twenty pounds. Ava spun around when I told him to fuck off.

"It was someone named Yuri," Allegra said, taking the knife. She tried and failed to cut through her ankle ties.

"Yuri?" Ava looked to the rest of us for confirmation.

"Yuri," Laura declared, hands patiently outheld for her turn with the knife. "Yes, it was him." Xavier said the same, and so did I. Yuri, it was Yuri.

Most galling of all, he was right about using the name Přem. When we swore to this new name, "Yuri," it must have sounded as if we were trying to populate the train with various baleful spirits. But I really don't know. I keep trying to allow for the doubts Ava must have had, but I still think that in her place I would have listened to us and believed us, just believed us. I would've done that first and then got the details in due course.

Though as Laura later pointed out, even if Ava had believed us, what could she have done about it? She still couldn't see the fucker. And she'd already written that trying to behave as if he was visible to her hadn't worked at all.

Once all four of us were unbound, Laura hobbled over to the kitchen table for her walkie-talkie. After minutes of white noise, she asked Ava: "But where are they, the maintenance team?"

"They said something about going for a walk along the coast. Understandably, they didn't like you kicking them off the train without telling them why."

"OK, but. The entire maintenance team?"

"It's a close-knit crew, Laura."

First aid kits were fetched out of a cupboard, tea was drunk, and strategies were signalled with our eyes. From the lounge area, Yuri surveyed us with—well, the diving mask obscured his expression. But he gave a grunt of contentment. Plus, wetsuits reveal all: he had a hard-on.

Ava watched us too. She watched as we gingerly rotated our ankles and jiggled our fingers. She was no longer annoyed with us—in fact I think it's not an understatement to say that she looked miserable.

The two mongooses followed Ava into her sleeping compart-ment. Allegra showed every sign of wanting to go with them . . . to the extent that she began to crawl in that direction on her hands and knees. But Xavier whispered to her that she should just wait for the maintenance team. And then Ava, not in bed after all, began to play "For Přemysl at Night."

She played it differently; this time the notes were granular and we heard them as hordes. A furore in the soil that buried us alive. Still, we sank with our arms wrapped around each other. Allegra, Laura, Xavier, and me. The less Ava liked us as a "we," the tighter our hold. After a couple of moments, Allegra said: "Ow." There were several issues her "ow" could have been addressing, but her main one was that Laura's walkie-talkie was digging into her back.

Ava stopped playing.

"What's that? What are you whispering among yourselves?" she called out.

"Nothing, Ava. Sorry."

A scratchy silence followed, and for a few minutes it seemed as if Ava was going to leave that silence exactly as it was. She put on a sleeping mask. I saw this reflected in the carriage window across from her cabin, and it struck me as ominous. I'm not sure I'm going to be able to articulate reasons . . .

Partly it was Ava's expression. The grim line her mouth was set in as she pulled the silk down over her closed eyelids. Partly it was Yuri's reaction from his ringside seat, the way he rubbed his hands together. After about a minute just sitting quietly with her hands on her thighs, Ava elevated her arms and played from memory, beginning all over again.

A jumble of inner and outer matters followed: The clack of the exterior door as maintenance team members tried to access the carriage from the platform. Ava concluding her performance and walking blindfolded through our midst as we struggled upright, too timid to satisfy our craving to catch at her clothing. With the exception of Laura, we murmured, "Beautiful . . . Ava, that was really beautiful . . ." I remember wondering, mid-grovel, why we were being like this, but from this point in time I think we already knew what had just happened and were hoping against hope that it could be remedied.

The maintenance team redoubled their knocking efforts, but Ava stopped halfway to the exterior door and turned in our direction. "Guys?" she said. Her hands went to the sleeping mask, then she scowled. "What now? They ran off while I was playing?"

"Ms. Kapoor," Laura said, in a very loud and very firm voice. "We were here listening, Ms. Kapoor. I assure you I would have run away if I had the strength."

"Rude," Ava said. "So fucking rude."

We relaxed. Until she called out to us again. "Guys? Seriously? I'm giving you three seconds to answer me. I don't feel like playing hide-and-seek right now. Three . . ."

Yuri sniggered. "Ah, so this is how it happens," he said, getting up and walking over to Ava. He turned so he was facing us, just as Ava was.

"Two," Ava said.

We bellowed in unison, at the top of our lungs:

"AVAAAAAAAAA ..."

"MS. KAAAAAPOOOOOOOOR ..."

Allegra Yu didn't join us. She looked out of the window, in a trance, as if we were already on our way home.

"One."

Ava lifted the sleep mask, and Yuri said: "Ciao, bambini. You're all screwed." That was the last we saw or heard of him. A very literal "missed his departure whilst blinking" situation.

We shouted and waved (somewhat feebly) as Ava walked backward, checking her sleeping compartment. Two sleeping mongooses in there, but that was all. She checked Laura's compartment, and Allegra's, even moving the pillows around on the beds. Several times her eyes met ours directly, but no, no sign of recognition, nothing.

"For fuck's sake, Ava ..."

"AVA, PLEAAAAASE. Please!"

"Four years we've lived together, Ms. Kapoor. Four years."

"I'd have heard it if they'd left ... I'd have heard it, wouldn't I?" she said, flopping down on the ground next to Allegra.

Silently, Allegra turned to her. They almost bumped noses. Silently, Allegra took in Ava's face, her gaze falling like a wave of honey. A leave-taking look. Ava kissed her; then, as the pounding at the platform door grew frantic, she jumped up to let the maintenance team in.

Allegra stood up too: "Wh—Ava? You can—?"

Ava gave her the smile. The really very wonderful smile. "I can what?"

She could, and she did. She'd unseen us. But not Allegra.

Why didn't I (or Laura, or Xavier) force bodily contact? Why didn't one of us tap Ava on the shoulder, for instance, or stand in her path and insist that she take notice of us? We didn't dare to. As for why we didn't dare . . . you wouldn't have either! Suppose your finger passed through the shoulder you'd presumed to tap, straight through, as if that shoulder were a mere hologram? Or suppose some overwhelmingly anti-magnetic sensation prevented your finger from descending onto the target shoulder? Let's just suppose and suppose and suppose, and never find out for ourselves what life turns into after that decisive a failure to connect . . .

When *The Lucky Day* got going again, it blasted along the nighttime rails like a getaway train.

All the breakup advice I've read advocates drawing boundaries of your own. At some point you have to become as unavailable to your rejecter as they are to you. So here are my red lines:

No thinking of the infirmary car that was in the very last carriage, beyond the bazaar carriage. I'm discarding the memory of lying in there that very night with Xavier and Laura and Allegra, lying there two by two, drinking in the ether of that antiseptic haven and trying not to think about what's going to happen to us now that we'd been unseen. Let's forget the way Allegra offered all three of us a shoulder to cry on but we were too bitter to take her up on it. I won't say which one of us told her, "This isn't something you have to worry about, Allegra. Yet." There's no use revisiting Allegra's semi-elated expression as she agreed with us regarding the "yet" bit; I won't wonder whether she considered that uncertainty a perk.

Nor do I want to talk about how Ava came into the Stojaspal inheritance the very next day. Conjecture's almost too tempting. If I gave in, my guess would be that the question of Karel Stojaspal's son wasn't even raised. I'd wager that the sanity trap lay in Ava's own raising of the question. Since she didn't, everything quietly continued as she perceived it. That is, as if this Přem person had never been.

And I certainly don't want to bitch about Árpád Montague XXX and the slightly apologetic yet maximally dedicated way he pretended to unsee us. He only did it because Chela did. I'm enclosing the last time I saw Árpád in a square of fat red lines . . .

It was in the infirmary carriage. Ava had just visited Allegra with a care package: chicken soup, a pair of fresh white trainers, etc. We, the soupless and white trainer–less, had glared and glowered throughout this visit, to very little effect aside from dispelling surplus feeling. You always imagine that the things said about you behind your back will have some intensity to them, but Ava spoke so airily of our departure that it was highly unsatisfactory to hear ourselves talked about. The mongooses were in attendance; apparently respects must be paid to Ava's favourite . . . and Árpád gave me a single backward glance as they were leaving the carriage. One look before running to catch up with Chela Kapoor. Whipped. Whipped! Atrociously so.

21.

What I do like to remember is the sight of Do Yeon-ssi waiting for us at the station, drinking a soju milkshake with her sunglasses on. She was sitting on the suitcase I'd left behind, and when she saw us come staggering along the platform with Xavier's suitcase, she said: "So my nephews are back. My nephews and . . . ?"

Laura sat down beside her.

"Shin Do Yeon, meet Laura De Souza," Xavier said. "Your niece until further notice."

I clocked Do Yeon-ssi clocking Laura's expertly concealed black eye. The auntly eyebrows rose a fraction of a millimetre, and she rolled up her sleeves. After three solemn rounds of "paper, scissors, stone," during which both she and Laura unwaveringly chose "scissors." Do Yeon-ssi said: "Well, this aunt has been waiting a long time for you, niece. But . . . no Árpád? No Yuri?!"

We held the swiftest frown ballot imaginable, Xavier, Laura, and I. Laura was elected official spokesperson. "Well, Ms. Shin. We'll have to tell you later on, piece by piece."

Do Yeon-ssi looked at us, then at the swiftly departing *Lucky Day*. "I see . . ."

She did, I think.

It was sunny out, so we walked home along grassy lanes. Good weather is exciting for the sociable yet self-conscious; it's a chance to discuss something positive without appearing to boast or pry. Laura De Souza took us by surprise with the amount she had to say about the weather. I think we surprised ourselves on the same front. Still unsure if we'd truly made it to the end of that honeymoon of ours, we exchanged weather-based pleasantries with all and sundry. Little things concerned us: Xavier and I had just found we'd both been locked out of our Instagram accounts. Probably an unrelated hacking spree . . .

It's early days yet: only a month since we got unseen. And so far everything—even the ongoing Instagram exile—has been supremely pedestrian. I, for one, welcomed the recent rainy spell. On strolls around the village I'm yet to tire of the thrill of leaving footprints in the mud.

April 14, 2019–November 23, 2019
Prague, Czechia

Acknowledgments

Thank you, Dr. Cieplak. Thank you, Tracy Bohan. Thank you, Petr Onufer. Thank you, Jin Auh. Thank you, Mike Baugh. Thank you, Alison Fairbrother. And Sarah McGrath—thank you.